LITTLE OSCAR

By the author:

THE BARRIER
VENDETTA MOUNTAIN
LITTLE OSCAR

LITTLE OSCAR

a novel of erotic realism

by

Carmen Anthony Fiore

TOWNHOUSE PUBLISHING
Princeton, New Jersey

Published by
Townhouse Publishing
301 N. Harrison Street
Building-B, Suite 115
Princeton, NJ 08540

Manufactured in the United State of America

First printing

Library of Congress Cataloging-in-Publication Data

Fiore, Carmen Anthony, 1932–
  Little Oscar : a novel of erotic realism / Carmen
Anthony Fiore.
    p.   cm.
  ISBN 0–939219–04–2 (pbk. : alk. paper) : $7.95
  I. Title.
PS3556.I57L58 1988
813'.54—dc19   88–10219
                                                    CIP

This book is dedicated to
PENNY JOHNSON FERRI,
my first reader who always
keeps me editorially straight.

Life is like a fire; it begins
in smoke, and ends in ashes.

ARAB PROVERB

PART I

Chapter 1

Debbyanne could barely shut the door of the older
model pickup truck, when the contractions gripped her
like a twisting hard fist deep inside her, then released
and undulated in wavelike spasms downward toward
her pelvis. They were coming with more regularity now.
She didn't tell the confused driver why she wanted to
get out on Creek Road, a thousand feet from the
Pleasanton-Mt. Lebanon Road intersection. All she
could muster was a faint smile and a wave of her limp
right hand as the truck pulled away, leaving an acrid
stink of blue-tinted exhaust fumes in its wake.

From that vantage point she could see the barn-red
farm buildings through the road's flanking strip of
naked-limbed maple and oak trees, without being seen
herself. She was grateful there wasn't any snow on the
ground, being a mid-December day with low gray
clouds above, threatening rain, snow, or worse, sleet.
She had worried about the weather ever since leaving

Capital City earlier in the morning, some ninety miles to the south.

And the bouncing ride in the tractor trailer cab, during the entire trip, had been hard on her lower spine. But she had to consider herself lucky, finding a truck driver who was going north at the diner, where she had stopped for breakfast. Making it to Creek Road in one ride in her condition was a godsend.

Debbyanne waited until the driver had turned right at the Pleasanton-Mt. Lebanon Road intersection ahead and disappeared from sight, before she moved off Creek Road into the trees. It was an effort to collect herself after those last labor pains. She straightened her back and walked slowly with one deliberate step at a time over the uneven branch- and leaf-strewn ground, wincing from the now steady ache in her lower spine.

She rebuttoned the top button of her blue cloth coat, a gift from the last lady she'd housecleaned for. The garment had seen better days, pockets ripped and the two lower buttons missing, which didn't matter in her bloated condition, and thankfully didn't impede her lumbering progress.

When she came to the familiar split-rail wooden fence that flanked the farm's back acreage, she paused and held her protruding stomach with her small hands, then breathed deeply, exhaling vapory plumes from her nose in the chilled December air.

The next series of contractions proved more severe than the last. Her time was getting nearer. She had to get to one of the sheltering farm buildings—and soon. Her dropped front pressed tightly against the maroon maternity top and mint-green cardigan sweater, more hand-me-downs.

An occasional cold breeze worked its icy fingers into the tears and crevices of her clothing and under the knee-length wool maternity skirt. The bare skin on her calves above the drooping white anklets was already

numb. She wished she could bend over and rub some life back into her legs.

After the pains subsided, she dislodged the top and middle rails and stepped awkwardly over the remaining lower rail, lifting her swollen legs one at a time like a stiff-legged elephant, and feeling just as big and cumbersome.

Each step over the rough-surfaced field, its green winter rye grass three inches high, was sheer agony for Debbyanne. Her breath came in rapid, hissing drafts. Inhaling the crispy cold air stung her lungs. But no way would she have let the truck driver drop her off at the farmhouse. The doorstep scene would have been a little too tense in front of him, a stranger. She still had some pride left.

The privacy of the tractor shed would be good enough for now. She'd do it all by herself—in there. What she had learned in the natural birth classes in Capital City would get her through it. Afterwards, she'd face them.

Between rest stops for air and to weather the gripping uterine contractions, which were coming with quicker, fiercer regularity now, it took what seemed like an hour to make it to the rearmost utility building, which was out of view of the farmhouse that faced toward the Pleasanton-Mt. Lebanon Road.

And when she finally approached the tractor shed, with a heavy sigh of relief, she felt a sudden wetness running down her legs, soaking her oversized panties, socks, and the ground beneath her. She hurriedly opened the wooden, ten-foot-wide door just enough to sidle in, with her bigness brushing against its splintery boards. Two steps inside, she smelled long-remembered odors of gasoline, oil-stained, trampled dirt, aged wood and greasy rags. She found a canvas tarpaulin in good condition next to the tractor, and spread it out for a bed on the damp earthen floor. It was cold and dark inside

the familiar building, but she appreciated the shelter it afforded. She had played tractor driver and farmer in it as a little girl, sitting high up on the tractor's seat and turning the wide steering wheel, while humming motor sounds; back when the shed was in better condition, and she couldn't see light streaming through the spaces in the roof.

After another deep, drawing contraction of her uterus, Debbyanne hurriedly spread the clean towel she'd been carrying inside her sweater on the tarpaulin. She pulled up her wool skirt and slid the dampened panties down her legs, stepping out of them where they fell, then lowered herself slowly and awkwardly, feeling like a wounded, dying buffalo, onto the clean white towel. Exhausted from the effort, she lay back full-length on the towel and the tarpaulin, breathing heavily, as if she couldn't get enough oxygen into her lungs, and waited for the final pains that she knew would be coming—and soon.

Five minutes later, the sharp, ripping, pulling spreading pain stretched her back bow-taut on the tarpaulin. She let out her first unrepressed banshee cry. Then she arched her back, inhaling deeply, using her abdominal muscles to help push the baby out faster, the way the nurse at the natural birth classes had instructed, before relaxing to help with the next onslaught of labor contractions, and the next, and the next, and the next, until the baby came out of her. Confrontation with her parents would be easy after that.

She was spread open like a rose at full bloom. A man's fist could be shoved up her. The pains were only a few minutes apart now. The baby was coming right on schedule that Friday, December 16, 1966, just as the young clinic intern had predicted, a mid-December birth.

Despite the breathing, the pushing, and the self-control, it was the final knife-stabbing pains to get the

4

baby's head out of her, as if she'd been spread apart
with a crowbar, that were too much to suppress. She let
go of a Tarzanlike, King-of-the-Jungle wail, expelling
the hurt as best she could. Then it was breathe in
deeply to push, grunt, scream, twist and turn, writhing
like a sick, bloated cow on her blood-soaked white towel
and grimy tarpaulin.

Debbyanne knew in the end she'd have to help the
baby to come out completely. But first she had to push
with the contractions to get the baby's shoulders free,
then find the strength to prop herself up and get the
rest of him out. And for her final effort she held her
ankles and arched her back, with her head digging into
the tarpaulin. She kept her knees high, bare legs and
lower torso exposed to the cold, which she didn't feel
now, nor mind. It was the pain that was all-consuming.

With one last, bloodcurling screech, she made it.
The baby hung half out of her. When the numbing pain
eased momentarily, she used her arms and elbows to
raise herself, easing her bulk around in a half circle to
rest her upper back and shoulders against the big tractor tire. Once supported, she used shaky hands to ease
the baby the rest of the way out of her. It was soft and
slippery from the blood and mucous, the skin wrinkled,
but hers—all hers.

Sweat-drenched, despite the cold and her seminude
condition, Debbyanne stretched her legs outward and
lay the baby between them on the bloody towel. He was
still attached to her by the accordion-looking umbilical
cord. She studied him a moment, counting his fingers
and toes. Then she smiled at his tiny, scrunched-up
ears. He had a fine tan coloring, where he wasn't covered with blood. And he was alive and shivering from
the shocking cold on his glistening nakedness. She patted him on the back. When he let out his first howl, she
flinched. But he soon settled into a steady, protesting
cry. She was relieved. He was scrawny-looking, with

skinny chicken legs, but he was hers—all hers. She slid him carefully up her stomach to rest against her bosom, covering him with her coat.

"That's it, cry yourself alive, little Oscar Wellington Hodges, the Third."

Debbyanne let her own tears flow, forgetting for the moment her body's spreading hurt, its total muscular fatigue and complete physical exhaustion as she cuddled her new son closer to her milk-swollen breasts.

Morley and Sarah Rockland stumbled down the back farmhouse shed steps, jostling each other to get the lead in their search to find out what the screams were all about. Farmers too long, they knew it couldn't be one of their stock. It had to be human, and on their property, to be heard through doors and windows closed for that time of the year. The continuous crying sound told them just where to look, after the screaming had stopped. And having been parents, they knew the sound of an infant's cry when they heard it.

"Good God all mighty!" Morley Rockland blurted out in his husky, cough-wracked voice, after throwing open the tractor shed door.

"Debbyanne!" Sarah Rockland piped in a high nasal pitch.

"Meet your new grandson," Debbyanne replied, opening her coat and offering her parents a better look.

They stepped closer, squinting at him in the poor light.

"You never wrote you got married," her father said. Then after spreading out his arms like Christ on the Cross, and looking around the shed, he added, "Why in here?"

"I had to do this myself, without any flak from you, or her," Debbyanne replied, glancing sideways at her mother. "I never married his father, just lived with him a short time." Her delivery was slow, with frequent

pauses for rest. When she finished, she looked directly up at her father.

But Sarah Rockland replied, "So now you've got an illegitimate child on your hands . . . and ours, too."

"Right, Mother, but remember, he's still your grandson."

"Don't like his looks," her father said, leaning closer to stare at the baby.

Sarah Rockland followed suit, then asked, "His father wasn't a Negro, was he?"

"He was light-skinned, but you'd still consider him a black man." Debbyanne held up her new son for her mother to hold. "Help me get up," she said to her father. And once up, with her legs wobbly and her pelvis feeling as if someone had shoved a hot poker up inside her, she used the tractor wheel to brace her back and steady herself. The umbilical cord that still stuck out of her blocked her skirt from falling past her knees. After she took her baby back from her mother, she used the coat lapels to cover him again. "I haven't had any contractions yet to get rid of the afterbirth. I might need a doctor to get it all out now."

Her parents didn't reply, just nodded somberly, their mouths unsmiling.

And when she thought she was ready for walking, Debbyanne said, "We can clean this mess up later. Get us into the house. I don't want my son getting sick from the cold." But after only a few steps, despite the support of her parents, she almost collapsed. After a minute of rest, she added, "Let's keep going, I'll be all right."

They began walking as a trio again, with Morley Rockland wearing a scowl on his weather-beaten, seamed face that looked like aged leather, and with Sarah Rockland's reddened eyes tearing, eyelids blinking rapidly.

"We'll have to call Old Doc Harding to cut the cord and get the afterbirth out of you, before infection sets

7

in." Sarah Rockland's tremulous voice was near breaking.

Debbyanne nodded and pulled the coat collar over her baby's head. The odorous blend of blood and mucous lifted off his small body and shiny head. She held him closer to her, arms shaking from the effort, while limping along with her parents' support at either side. The farmhouse inched closer with each step. Her trembling knees and shaking legs vibrated like marsh reeds in a stiff wind.

Walking on the hard ground jostled her, sending a burning sensation deep into her groin. The dull ache in her lower spine increased to sharp pain. She wanted to cry, and let herself fall down and rest; but instead she allowed herself to stop occasionally to get her breath, regaining enough strength to walk another ten feet. She was determined to make it to that aged clapboard farmhouse of her youth. Its gray paint was dirty and peeling, but inside was warmth, security and life for her son.

"Wait till Old Doc Harding sees the baby. A nigger bastard, yet." Morley Rockland muttered mostly to himself, with dark, juicy tobacco stains decorating the corners of his wide mouth, while he stared down at his mud-stained workboots.

"Just remember, Dad, he's still your grandson."

Morley Rockland grunted like a pig foraging for roots.

Sarah Rockland cried softly, the tears running down her puffy cheeks unwiped.

Debbyanne Rockland smiled down at her son, who shivered in her arms while he sucked contentedly on his thumb, his buttonlike eyelids closed tightly.

Chapter 2

Debbyanne listened obliquely to the familiar bucolic sounds of spring that first Monday morning in May as she spooned strained apricots out of a jar into Little Oscar's opened, eager mouth. Chirping robins made wing-fluttering charges over choice worm-hunting territory on the farmhouse's side lawn. And whenever the breeze picked up, the nearest maple's tender new leaves brushed softly against the gray clapboard siding and the kitchen's black asphalt shingle roof. Overhead a flight of crows cawed flying instructions to one another. A cow bellowed plaintively from the barn. Egg-laying chickens clucked incessantly in their coops. Pigs grunted and snorted in their sty, while foraging the daily slop.

Whenever she breathed deeply, she could smell the sweet odor of freshly cut rye field grass wafting through the opened screened windows, vying for contention with the dank smell of plowed earth that had been recently machine-raked and seeded after the April rains had

stopped a week ago. But when a whiff of barnyard manure intruded, she frowned and held her nose.

Debbyanne remembered hearing these same sounds and smelling similar odors during her growing-up years on the farm. She wanted her son to know them, before they left for good. When? She couldn't predict. The distant future always loomed vague and unsure to her, making it difficult to plan ahead, or try to manipulate her present life to assure happiness and success were forthcoming. Success at what?—she wasn't sure. But she thought she'd be able to recognize happiness when she found it.

She would have to put up with her parents for now, and with the township welfare people who grudgingly sent over a weekly food order via the local general store in the towny crossroads part of their rural community, thanks to Doc Harding's recommendation.

The farm-bred bureaucrats were frugal to the core. She knew that not everybody who applied for help got it. To them anything smacking of welfare was tantamount to socialism and bordered on sloth. Personal independence and family solidarity in taking care of their own were the accepted foundations they built their world on. Her parents shared similar views and attitudes. So her being on the local public dole was repugnant to them. But they were hurting financially. It was obvious. The farm had deteriorated. The farmhouse looked downright seedy, and the farm's equipment broke down daily. Her father spent as much time being a mechanic as being a farmer. His fingernails always had semicircles of black grease caked under them. And she couldn't help but notice how her parents had aged in just the year's time she had been away.

Doc Harding, eighty if a day, family friend and physician, knew their situation. He had insisted the township help support Debbyanne and her son while they lived on the farm. Her parents had reluctantly agreed,

letting their stiff-backed pride take a step backward. Debbyanne was in no position to argue, weak and recuperating and worried about her son's chance of surviving after being born in such unsanitary conditions in the cold tractor shed. She also hurt inside knowing how her parents felt about him. At least with the township's help, her parents couldn't claim an intolerable burden had been foisted on them. Besides, Doc Harding never overcharged for her visits with Little Oscar. But she was still relieved that he was a good baby and didn't disturb her parents. He slept all night and cried only when wet, messy, or hungry.

And could he eat. She loved feeding him. He always beamed his patented, toothless, pink-gum smile for her at mealtime, or wiggled and waved his arms when he knew he was getting his bottle of milk.

It hurt Debbyanne that her mother and father never picked him up and held him in their arms. Soon he'd be six months old. It was one more mark against them. She wouldn't forget it, nor forgive, not her.

Debbyanne's thoughts were interrupted when her father came thumping into the kitchen with his heavy leather workboots. She fed the last of the pasty apricot mush to Little Oscar without looking up, or acknowledging his presence in any other way. But she couldn't ignore the strong odor of pig and cow dung lifting off his boots. She tried to take shallow breaths, while keeping her attention focused on her baby.

Her mother was silently stirring yet another pot of stew by the iron cooking stove that always made the kitchen unbearable in summer.

"Did you tell her, yet?" her father asked her mother, who remained mute and just shook her head no, getting a pursed expression on her puffy face. Debbyanne remembered it was a sure sign of uneasiness on her mother's part.

"Tell me what?" she asked.

"We called the state welfare people. They're sending over a social worker today," her father replied, his crackling hoarse voice sounding as if sandpaper were scraping against his voice box inside his thick bull neck.

The spoon fell out of Debbyanne's hand, landing on the wooden tray in front of Little Oscar. She pulled the highchair closer and used a damp washcloth to wipe his mouth. After a glaring pause, she asked, "Exactly what for?"

"About him," her father replied.

"Can't you say, Oscar, or Little Oscar, like any other grandfather would?"

"For Christ's sake, why did you have to name him OSCAR?"

"It was his father's name."

Morley Rockland made a face that deepened the creases in his heavily seamed skin from his protruding lower-lipped mouth to the crow's-feet on his temples and the sagging chicken skin under his eyes. The lines looked as if etched with a knife. Then he took out a folded pouch of chewing tobacco from his denim jacket pocket and fingered out a pinch of the dark brown shredded leaf. And with the deftness of a brain surgeon, he placed it in the left side of his mouth between cheek and gum, before he asked Debbyanne, "Couldn't you give him a white man's name? It's still not too late to change it. You never did register his birth at the township hall. Old Doc Harding can be the witness and attending physician. You've got to do that sometime, you know. So you can still name him something better, nicer to say, even."

"Your father's right, Debbyanne. You could name him—Jonathan—after my father," her mother said with a whine to her voice, while standing at her post next to the cooking stove.

"His name is Oscar Wellington Hodges, the Third, after his father, who was a very nice man and treated me decent. And he died a tragic death protecting me from some white street hoodlums. It's the least I can do in his memory. And I don't want to talk anymore about that unhappy moment in my life ever again. It's too upsetting. Understand? So let's consider his name settled, if and when I bother to get his birth officially registered."

"I was only suggesting. Old Doc Harding can do it for you."

"It's not appreciated."

"Excuse me."

"You're not excused. Believe me, you're not."

"All right, we'll forget the name business. Now when the social worker comes . . ." her father began.

"That's another thing," Debbyanne interrupted. "Exactly why is this state social worker coming here?"

"I told you. About him. Your Oscar."

"Was his name that hard to say?"

Her father grunted and retreated to the stove where he poured himself a cup of coffee from the simmering metal pot, then sat at the table across from Debbyanne. Its once shiny varnished surface was dulled and scarred from decades of knife and fork gougings and food and liquid spills.

"I'm still waiting for somebody to tell me why this social worker is coming here."

Her father glanced at her mother, who looked down into the steaming stew pot, stirring the concoction at a faster rate with the long wooden spoon.

"Do I have to guess?"

"You're still underage. You got no husband to support you. No income of your own. And we're not making enough farming to make ends meet ourselves. Just barely holding our own, keeping the farm up and pay-

13

ing the taxes. Good thing Old Doc Harding put the word in to get you some help from those snippy township welfare people. I didn't want any, but I guess we had no choice. Your brothers and sisters are no help. Never write or send money. Scattered all over God's creation, from California to Florida, thanks to the schooling I paid for. And got no thanks in return. Children don't give a damn about their parents these days, like in our time. Don't respect their parents; don't even respect each other."

After Morley Rockland stopped talking, he stared with lowered eyelids into his deep-bowled ceramic cup, then lifted it slowly to his lips and drank noisily, sucking in air with the coffee.

"So what else is new?" Debbyanne said.

"We can't see you—and us—tied down to raising him. I mean, Oscar."

"And? . . ."

"We thought maybe we could get the state social worker to come out here and explain about adoption for him . . . I mean, Oscar. So he can end up living in a nice house with a nice young white couple who want a kid, and who'll give him a decent life."

"A nice young white couple?"

"Sure. Niggers don't adopt. They breed like rabbits themselves. So don't say nothing about his father being a nigger. If the social worker asks, just say he was a Latin, like maybe Puerto Rican, or even better, Eyetalian."

"You want me to lie in order to give up Oscar? Having him was the only important thing I've ever done in my life, so far. He's my baby. He was no hand-me-down, neither. He belongs to me. He's all mine. I made him inside me, and gave my blood to have him, suffered pain like you'd never believe. And now I'm supposed to give him up like he was damaged merchandise? Like hell I will!"

14

Her father banged his large-knuckled right fist down on the hard maple table, spilling coffee from his rocking cup onto the nicked surface. "You're talking nonsense. You can't afford a baby. How you going to work and raise him at the same time? What job can you get? What the hell can you do for a living? We're not going to be around forever to bail you out. And the township won't feed you two forever. You got no choice. You've got to give him up. So be sensible, talk to the social worker, without being snotty, like you are with me and your mother. Let her explain about adoption. You'll see, it's the best thing for you and him." Her father pointed a shortened forefinger at her, then his stubby thumb toward Little Oscar. And after nodding toward her mother, he added, "And us, too."

"You're right, it's the best thing for you two. But not for me."

"Think about the trouble you'll have raising him . . . I mean, Oscar. You'll soon come to your senses and agree with us."

"You just want to get rid of him because he's part black and illegitimate; and you're afraid he'll cost you money again for the doctor visits."

Morley Rockland nodded slowly, his face a mask of lines on swollen red skin.

"Your father's right, Debbyanne."

"It's not a question of being right, Mother. We're dealing with my feelings, and my baby's future. And how about love?"

"Just talk to the social worker," her father replied. "She'll make you see the light. Then you'll want to do the best thing for him . . . I mean, Oscar."

"I'll bet she will," Debbyanne said, reaching over and stroking her son's tiny-fingered hands. And when he dribbled spit down his chin, she quickly wiped it away with a washcloth.

"If you give him up now, it'll be easier to pass him

off as white. But if you wait too long, he just might start looking more like his father. Then it'll get a lot tougher to find him a nice white home."

"And? . . ."

"Who wants a mixed black and white baby, today? Nobody, that's who."

"He's my baby and I love him. I want to keep him. Can't I convince anybody around here of that?"

"You're nuts!"

"It must run in the family."

"Maybe a good slap in the mouth'll teach you some respect." Her father slammed his cup down and spilled more coffee on the kitchen table.

"Morley, please, you promised not to lose your temper," her mother said.

"Always the slap. Never understanding. I can still feel the sting on my cheeks from the last ones you dished out, the night I ran away."

"But you came home. Must not of hurt that much."

"I must be a fool, or a glutton for punishment, or maybe a little of both." Debbyanne turned away from her father as the tears welled up in her eyes. She swallowed the tightness rising in her throat as she reached over the highchair's wooden tray and took Little Oscar's soft hands in hers. She held them a long time, while he cooed and slobbered onto his cloth bib and tried to make sounds that came out *da da* and *ma ma.*

Later in the afternoon, with Little Oscar on her lap, Debbyanne sat quietly in the living room's wing chair, an overstuffed leftover from the early depression thirties. Its faded, original dyed wool covering was hidden under a solid brown cotton throw cover. It took up the entire corner farthest from the front door flanked by a brass ashtray stand to the right, and a three-shelf mahogany veneer knickknack wall piece to the left dis-

playing assorted glass, porcelain and ceramic figurines.

Her parents were ensconced on the three-cushioned sofa like reigning king and queen, sitting bolt upright on their thrones. It was the most imposing piece of furniture in the room, located across from Debbyanne, but closer to the front door. And it was from the same depression era, needing a protective flowery print cotton throw cover to hide thirty-five years of wear.

Oily light spread weakly outward through brownish-white paper lampshades from two porcelain table lamps squatting lumplike on mahogany veneer end tables.

The faded, worn brown wool area rug smelled of age and dust; and wrinkled prints inside dark wood frames decorated the yellowing wallpapered walls.

Debbyanne never liked the living room when a little girl, and decided once again that she still didn't like it as she waited for the interrogation to start by the visitor from the state.

Mrs. Brownel had stated that she loved old rocking chairs and chose to sit in the creaking high-backed Boston rocker catty-corner from Debbyanne and her parents. She filled it to capacity, making the oak wood creak louder under her bulk, whenever she moved in the slightest.

Debbyanne wondered if the fiftyish-looking woman ever ran a comb through her mass of unruly, brittle gray hair on that big, wide head of hers. Everything about Mrs. Brownel was big and wide. Debbyanne could see the lines of her corset straining against the woman's dark blue suit skirt. She had to contain the urge to laugh out loud, listening to the social worker puffing for air as she got her records straight in the manila folder on her heavy, thickset thighs, a formidable lap by anyone's standards.

The introductions and seating had taken only a few minutes, but now the dead-air silence was getting awk-

ward. And when the woman finally began speaking, Debbyanne almost applauded.

"Your parents are concerned about your being underage, Debbyanne." Her voice was breathy and light. "And now, you're saddled with the enormous responsibility of caring for an infant. Especially since there's no father, and/or no husband available to share the burden, both socially and financially."

"I'm touched."

Mrs. Brownel reached in under the long-sleeved dark blue suit jacket and tugged at her bra strap hidden by a frilly white blouse, before adding, "And they asked me to explain the state's child care program, under which you sign over your baby's care for long-term foster home placement, and/or adoption procedures, where you give up custody of the baby entirely. They especially wanted me to explain the advantages to you of considering adoption."

Debbyanne didn't reply, just hugged Little Oscar closer to her, while he sucked his thumb and stared big-eyed at the imposing woman in the rocker.

"You are receiving local assistance now, but that won't last forever. You'll eventually be asked to apply for help under the federally sponsored Aid to Dependent Children program, which is administered by the county, if you want long-term financial assistance, which means regulated welfare pure and simple. Independent people like your parents have always found that repugnant. Sometimes pride can be an admirable trait in an age when it's rapidly losing its meaning, with so many able-bodied people on the public dole these days."

"You're telling me something I don't already know?"

Mrs. Brownel tugged at her bra strap again, then asked, "Have you considered adoption for the baby?"

"No."

"There are advantages for someone in your position."

"What advantages can there be?"

"The baby would have a mother and a father in a home situation. Parental love and care in a normal middle-class setting. Every child needs that kind of stability."

"Oscar gets all the love and care he needs from me."

"But he'll get the strength and guidance that only a father can give a son."

"I won't be single all my life. He'll get the father he needs."

"Most men wouldn't care to raise some other man's child."

"I'll find one who won't mind."

Mrs. Brownel squirmed her hippopotamus-size rear end in the confining rocker. "It would be a magnanimous, unselfish, sensible act on your part to give the baby up for adoption. There are so many white middle-class couples just waiting to adopt a baby and give it all the love and care a child could want, just as if the child were their very own."

"You would place Oscar with a white couple?"

"Yes, of course."

"Even if his father had been black?"

"His father . . . was a black man?"

"Yes he was. Don't let Oscar's blond hair fool you. If you look closer, it's got a kink to it. And Oscar didn't get his nice tan coloring on his own by sunbathing."

Mrs. Brownel brushed back her unruly hair, a ballpoint pen in her hand, before replying, "Your parents never mentioned his father being black."

"Does it complicate matters?"

"There isn't a big demand for children of mixed racial background. I'd have to find a nice light-skinned couple for Oscar. We still like to match the complexion of the child with the adopting parents. It might take

longer to place him. There is an experimental trend developing in placement services, placing mixed babies and children with understanding, liberal white couples. But it's still not the general procedure with us."

"I understand. But do they?" Debbyanne nodded toward her parents.

Sarah Rockland folded her heavy, flesh-sagging arms across her large bosom, leaning back deeper into the sofa.

Morley Rockland edged forward on the sofa cushion and aimed a shortened forefinger at Little Oscar. "We didn't think it made any difference, Mrs. Brownel. A baby's a baby, ain't he? And he's light enough to pass for white."

"Yes, he is a light-skinned baby."

"It could get sticky for the agency, passing a mixed baby off as all white, right, Mrs. Brownel?" Debbyanne said.

"You do understand, we'd have to reveal his entire background to any interested couple."

"Oh, we understand. But I'm not interested in foster home placement, or in permanent adoption, now or later."

"But your parents . . ."

"He's my baby, not theirs, and he's staying my baby."

"What's people going to say when he grows up and goes to school and starts looking more and more colored?" Her father's rough voice lashed at her like a bullwhip in full swing.

"Who gives a good goddamn what people say?"

"Now, Debbyanne, don't profane the Lord," her mother chimed in.

"What's your brothers and sisters going to say, when they come visiting us one of these Christmases? And the rest of the relatives we still got living around

these parts? Good thing the weather was bad this past Christmas. We didn't get a single visitor. Not a soul showed up. Snow scares company away these days. Even your children, scattered all over the country, become strangers soon as they leave home. Never phone to find out if you're still breathing, or just to say howdy, and ask about your health." And when Morley Rockland stopped talking, he sat back deeper into the sofa and shook his head slowly, while his lips closed to a tight pucker.

"We're wasting your time here, Mrs. Brownel," Debbyanne said in a flat, but determined voice. "Oscar's staying with me—forever!" she added with a tremulous edge to the last word. Debbyanne hugged her son closer to her and kissed the top of his head.

"Well, here's my card in case you should ever change your mind," Mrs. Brownel replied, squeezing herself up and out of the rocker.

Debbyanne glanced at the card, then dropped it on the top shelf of the knickknack stand nearby. She followed the social worker out of the house to the state car, still holding Little Oscar in her arms. But when she returned, her father blocked the front entrance.

"You did your goddarnest to foul up the chance to get rid of your nigger bastard, didn't you?" His smelly chewing tobacco breath spread around her like an invisible cloud of polluted air.

"Don't call your grandson names, and let me by. I don't have a sweater on Oscar, and it's starting to cool off outside."

"He's a smear on the Rockland name. We'll end up the talk of the county. The gossips'll have a field day picking us apart like we're no-account white trash from down in Creek Hollow, with their junk cars parked in their front yards. Most of 'em live in shacks and collect welfare of one kind or another. Never work. Just drink

21

and make more babies, and fight with one another when they get drunk, and keep the cops busy breaking it up."

Debbyanne squeezed by her father, but he followed her through the living room and dining room and into the kitchen, like a puppy dog tagging along behind its master. She ignored him and went about preparing a bottle of milk for her son.

"We want that baby out of this house. You'll phone Mrs. Brownel tomorrow and tell her you've thought it over and decided that adoption just might be the best thing for you and Oscar after all, having him live with a nice light-skinned couple who'll give him the best of everything."

Debbyanne filled a bottle with milk and dropped it into a small aluminum pot, added water, then put it on the cooking stove to take the chill out of the milk. The heat from the stove made her sweat. She pushed back her straw-colored hair from her face, letting it drape over her shoulders.

"You listening? I'm talking to you. You're still living under my roof. Eating food cooked on my stove. And I'm paying your doctor bills. So you'll take my orders and like it."

Debbyanne took the bottle out of the heated water and let it cool a moment, before testing the milk, squirting a few white drops on the back of her left hand. Then she brought it over to Little Oscar, who was lying in the old wooden crib near the open kitchen windows. At the sight of the bottle, he waved arms and legs and wiggled his abbreviated torso, his smile all gums and slobber.

When she returned to the sink, Debbyanne poured the hot water from the aluminum pot into it, then turned abruptly, as if on a turntable, her right arm flashing upward and forward, catapulting the lightweight utensil over the kitchen table at her father.

"Fuck you!" Debbyanne shouted, watching her father duck as the small pot bounced harmlessly off the kitchen wall behind him. Then pivoting, as if a soldier performing an about-face, she left the kitchen by the rear shed and joined her mother in the backyard to haul in the day's washing of Little Oscar's diapers.

Her father shouted from the back steps, "I'll break your goddarn neck, you ever try that again!"

"Not before I part your hair with a cleaver, you fucking bigot," Debbyanne mumbled into the soft diaper that smelled of fresh air, while she unhooked the wooden clothespins and took it off the rope clothesline. When she heard the rear shed door slam shut, she grinned to herself and unhooked another diaper.

"Debbyanne, what did you do to make your father so mad?" her mother asked.

"I threw a pot at him."

"You two will never get along."

"I guess not, as long as he thinks like he does."

"Both of you are as stubborn as mules."

"I may be a chip off the old stubborn block, but Oscar's mine. And he's staying mine. So I don't want to hear anymore about it." When Debbyanne finished speaking, she threw the last of the diapers into the plastic clothes basket, grabbed it up, and headed briskly for the house, leaving her mother squinting in the sunlight.

Chapter 3

Debbyanne lit the six-inch candle in the center of the chocolate layer cake, and sang "Happy Birthday" in an off-key voice to a beaming, thumb-sucking Little Oscar. Afterwards she had to help him blow out the flickering yellow-orange flame. She finished the ceremony with a hearty round of applause. Little Oscar joined in, but missed more than he connected with his small hands.

Her audience didn't participate. They just stood mutely on the other side of the kitchen table, observing with vacant expressions and dull, unmoving eyes, looking fully the part of reluctant bystanders.

Debbyanne glared at them. "Thanks for joining in and wishing my son a Happy Birthday. And thanks ever so much for the present you two didn't get him. Some grandparents." When she turned her attention back to her son, she gave him his first birthday present. Little Oscar embraced the Teddy Bear, tasting its furry ear, and squealed his delight.

Her parents remained silent, standing their ground, postures straight as two-by-fours, arms folded stiffly across their chests.

"You two really make terrific grandparents. He's a year old today, and how many times have either of you ever held him in your arms? Or kissed him? Even played with him? A big fat zero. That's how many times. And that's heartless. Taking out your prejudices on an innocent child." Debbyanne lifted her son out of his highchair, while he clutched the Teddy Bear to his chest. She carried him over to her father. "Here, hold him in your arms—for the first time. He's your grandson. And wish him a Happy Birthday." Debbyanne held Little Oscar out to her father, until her arms ached. But he remained unmoved, arms still folded across his chest, as if he never heard her. Deep frown lines rippled vertically across the ruddy skin on his wide forehead above his nose.

When Debbyanne offered her son to her mother to hold, she shook her head no, tightened the fold of her beefy arms across heavy, sagging breasts, hidden by a faded apron, its darker print design washed out and blurring into the dull background color.

Debbyanne couldn't stop the tears that trickled down her cheeks, dripping off her face to make damp spots on her red plaid flannel shirt. She returned Little Oscar to his highchair. And after wiping her face dry, she picked up a nine-inch stainless steel knife and stared at the cake on the kitchen table as if it were a victim on a sacrificial altar. The blown-out wax candle remained upright like a blue stone obelisk in the cake's dark brown icing.

"We don't want to hold him, kiss him, or wish him a Happy Birthday," her father said, his gravelly voice getting stronger with each word. "We want him out of this house. Didn't figure he'd be here this long. He's starting to look more colored. Probably end up a spitting

image of his father. And I don't know how many times we have to tell you before it sinks in, but we don't want a nigger kid in this house. So either you call Mrs. Brownel and give him up for adoption, or you can take him and go live someplace else. You don't appreciate nothing we do for you anyway. Same as your brothers and sisters."

Debbyanne slashed at the cake with the long knife, slicing through it quickly down to the glass dish underneath. She cut four slices and plopped them into separate glass dishes. Then she asked her parents, "At least you can have a piece of his birthday cake, can't you? Even if you can't wish him a Happy Birthday in your hearts, and with your mouths." Her voice sounded artificially hollow, as if coming from a loudspeaker instead of her mouth, while the words were hanging like strung beads in the stove-warmed kitchen air.

"I don't eat cake," her father replied.

"The way I've been putting on weight, I sure don't need any," her mother said.

"You'll both eat his birthday cake, if I have to shove it down your goddamn throats!" Debbyanne slid the glass plates over to her parents.

"We don't want any of his cake," her father replied, ambling gorillalike around the kitchen table. When he took hold of Debbyanne, it was with primate strength, clamping his hairy-knuckled fingers around her slim arm. "What we want is you calling Mrs. Brownel and getting your nigger bastard out of this house. You're getting too attached to him."

"He's my son, you idiot," Debbyanne replied, studying the broken blood vessels on her father's nose, and smelling his chewing tobacco breath, which made her want to vomit. "I should be attached to him. And you're his grandfather, so should you."

"Well, I ain't, and neither is your mother." Her fa-

ther squeezed harder, pinching the skin.

"I'm not calling anybody. And let go of my arm, you're hurting me."

His thick fingers dug deeper into her tender arm muscles and pressed against the bone.

"Let go of me, you fucking bastard!"

"Debbyanne, your language," her mother whined.

"You're calling Mrs. Brownel—now," her father said, dragging her toward the wall phone on the other side of the kitchen.

Debbyanne's vision dissolved to black. Her eyeballs became hot coals. She pulled against his strength, but couldn't stop him. She was like a helpless rag doll being dragged across the linoleum floor. And without conscious thought, she lunged at her father with the knife, ripping its sharp point into his baggy sweater sleeve. "I'll cut your heart out!" she screamed like an angry witch.

"Goddarn it," her father said, "you nicked my arm!" He let go of Debbyanne and reached into the cut sweater sleeve. And when he withdrew his hand, he showed the bloodstained fingertips to her.

"I'll do better than that," she said, slashing at her father again. But he grabbed her wrist and spun her around and forced her against the table, banging her arm against the hard surface until she dropped the knife. "You son-of-a-bitch!" she shouted into his florid-skinned face. "You're hurting me."

"I'll do more than hurt your goddarn arm."

The slaps were hard, stinging, and rapid. Debbyanne's face swelled to numb meat instantly. She dropped to her knees on the gritty linoleum floor. Her cheeks stung as if attacked by a thousand bees. She clung to the table's worn, rounded edge with weak hands. And when her mother shouted at her father to stop, it sounded as if the voice came from a sound cham-

ber. She looked up and watched her mother's blurry figure come between them.

"Stop, Morley! Before you really hurt her."

"I'll slap some goddarn sense into her empty head." Her father's voice was a sonic boom in her ears. "And I'll keep on slapping her, till she calls the social worker, like I told her to."

Debbyanne heard herself mumble, "When hell freezes over."

"Morley, are you crazy?" her mother said, pushing against her father's chest with extended arms.

Debbyanne struggled to get up, reeling as if drunk, her legs shaking inside hip-hugger jeans. She braced herself against the table's edge, using her arms and flattened palms for support. When she finally looked up at her father's red-veined eyes and weather-beaten face, she said, "You'll be a dead man a long time, before I'll ever give up my son."

"Then you'll leave this house and take your nigger bastard with you. And that's final. You hear me, smart ass?"

"I'll leave when I'm good and ready."

Her mother caught her father's swinging arm in midair, screaming, "Dear God, stop it, Morley!"

The atmosphere in the kitchen grew oppressive with the brittle silence that followed. Debbyanne stuffed her flannel shirt back into her jeans, then hurried over to Little Oscar and yanked him out of the highchair, fleeing seconds later up the back steps, seeking the sanctuary of her bedroom.

Once inside the small, square room, she locked the door and shoved a straight-backed, wooden-spoked chair up under the brass doorknob. When secure from invasion by her father, she retreated to her bed and lay there with her son imprisoned in her arms, while he still hugged his Teddy Bear. Debbyanne whispered into

his tiny ear, "We're leaving tomorrow morning, early. They sleep late on Sundays. We won't even say goodbye. I'm not letting any social worker take you away from me. You're mine." And when she stopped whispering, she had to finger-wipe the tears from her face.

Debbyanne lay on the bed for uncounted minutes, letting her pounding heart subside and her heated face and neck cool to normal, while Little Oscar's warm, soft body lay next to her, with the Teddy Bear between them. After awhile, he began exploring her face with his reed-thin, searching fingers. He studied her close up with his big, unblinking blue eyes, more pupil and iris than white, babbling all the while in his squeaky voice.

She could smell his Johnson's baby powder and baby breath, and didn't get up until she smelled another less pleasant telltale odor. She changed his diaper and put him in his crib at the foot of her bed.

Once up and active, Debbyanne packed a canvas overnight bag with toilet essentials for herself and her son, deciding to overdress herself and him with extra clothes she wanted to take along when they left in the morning. She'd get to the main state highway, even if she had to walk the five miles, carrying Little Oscar and the small bag. She couldn't stay in their house any longer. The hate for them had become a permeating oily mist, filling the unseen pores of her skin, leaving a film she could wash away only with time—and distance. If she stayed any longer, she'd end up killing her father, if he didn't kill her first.

Little Oscar needed a real mother, not a foster mother, or an adopted one. And she readily admitted to herself that she needed him just as much as he needed her. They'd make a new life in Capital City, blending in with its variety of people in the crowded neighborhoods of narrow streets and row houses. It was the nearest city, and the easiest to reach. She'd find someone there

she could be friendly with, as before. Anywhere would be better than living with parents who hated her son and rejected her.

Debbyanne stayed in her unheated bedroom for the rest of the afternoon, evening and night wrapped in a blanket while fully dressed. The only time she left it was to go to the bathroom, after her parents had gone to bed. She slept fitfully, with her senses primed to register every sound in the old house. She was glad to see daylight poke its long gray fingers into her darkened bedroom through the curtain-draped window that was angled toward the eastern horizon.

She forced herself out of bed, eyes burning from lack of sleep. Yawning and stumbling around her room like a drunken lady, she managed to dress herself and Little Oscar with extra layers of clothing as planned, to ward off mid-December's penetrating morning chill and rising dampness that she knew awaited her outside.

In the hallway, with one arm supporting her son, the other occupied with the overnight bag, she listened for sounds from her parents' bedroom that would indicate they were awake. A morning confrontation with her father was the last thing she wanted. She didn't continue toward the back stairs until she heard snoring coming from their room.

And since the coal- and wood-burning stove was not lit, the kitchen was bone-chilling cold. She could have only dry cereal with refrigerator-cold milk for herself, while feeding Little Oscar baby food out of a jar, packing the rest of his food into the overnight bag. After eating, it was time to go hunting. Debbyanne searched the cabinet farthest from the sink and found the ceramic cookie jar with the cracked lid. She removed fifty-five dollars in bills and sixty-seven cents in change and stuffed it all into her right pocket. She replaced the lid and set the jar back into its original place in the cabi-

net and closed the door. Returning to where Little Oscar sat in his highchair, she patted the bulge in her jeans and smiled with elfin glee.

It was only minutes later when Debbyanne let herself out the front door, moving carefully and quietly carrying the overnight bag and her son, whom she admonished to be quiet, when he squealed his infant's delight at being carried by her, while clutching his Teddy Bear with his baby-short arms. Her movements down the front porch steps were in exaggerated pantomime to keep from stumbling. She never looked back at the farmhouse, heading straight for the Creek Road intersection. It would be a five-mile trek down the country road to the main state highway that connected their rural area with Capital City to the south.

If she got a couple of quick, long-distance rides, they could be there by nightfall.

But the longer she hiked, carrying her son and the overnight bag, the more frequent were the rest stops. And what few cars and trucks that passed her during those early morning hours came from the opposite direction. So all she could do was walk and rest, whenever the ache in her arms became too much. She wore her old hand-me-down coat to ward off the penetrating breeze.

The flanking roadside scenery at that late in the autumn season was dismal. Dead brown leaves covered the ground. Naked trees stood stark and spindly against the gray sky. The rolling fields nearby were bleak and empty of crops. The landscape mirrored her mood. Little Oscar grew heavier by the hour, the overnight bag dead weight, numbing her arms, while her armpits dripped perspiration freely, despite the cold, breezy weather. The skin on her face was like untanned cowhide.

Debbyanne didn't make it to the four-lane concrete highway until well into the afternoon. Her feet burned inside her soft desert boots from the ungiving macadam surface of Creek Road. But the sight of the divided highway made the effort all worthwhile. Deciding to eat before hitching a ride, she fed Little Oscar first from one of his jars of baby food, then gave him a hunk of rye bread crust to massage his gums. She ate chicken breast white meat on rye bread, longing for something to drink as each dry mouthful slid roughly down her parched throat. But she chewed slowly and watched the highway's traffic, pleased with the volume, feeling confident she'd get a ride for them and they wouldn't have to spend the night outdoors.

When she finally crossed the seventy-foot-wide highway, she left Little Oscar on the grass shoulder and began thumbing for a ride immediately. Fifteen minutes later she got a tractor trailer to pull over to the shoulder and wait for her. She scooped up her son and the bag and ran to it. Puffing for breath, she had to stretch all five feet three inches of herself to reach the door handle. The driver helped push it open for her as she asked him, "Heading for Capital City?"

"Sure am, little honey, hop in."

His voice and delivery smacked of a Southern drawl.

"I've got a baby with me."

"I can see that. No sweat, darling. I love babies. Made a few myself."

Debbyanne arranged herself on the front seat beside the driver, the bag between her legs, with Teddy Bear-clutching Little Oscar on her lap, staring wide-eyed at the man beside them.

The dashboard-attached CB radio crackled alive and an electronic voice asked for directions to a town Debbyanne never heard of, as the driver double-clutched the huge vehicle forward, easing it back onto the highway.

Debbyanne gauged the driver's age range to be in the late thirties to the early forties. At least he wasn't repulsive-looking to her, like some of them. He wore a black leather vest over a long-sleeved, light blue checked shirt and gray work pants. His dark brown hair hung jauntily in a loose clump over his brow. A day's growth of black stubble covered his lean, long-jawed face and dimpled chin. His chestnut-brown eyes were active. Debbyanne sensed he liked what he saw in her, his thin-lipped smile breaking wider whenever their gazes met. But they drove mostly in silence, with the beige-brown dormant fields passing monotonously by them. Still, she had no illusions. There would be a price to pay for the ride. And she was willing to meet it in full. She had gone that route before.

She introduced herself by her first name only. The driver's name was Ben. His CB handle was Twenty Pounder, a private joke among his trucker friends, which aptly described a private part of his male anatomy. Debbyanne smilingly agreed it was good for a laugh, wondering when he'd make his first move at her. After he ate and refueled at the first truckers rest stop? She shrugged and sat back in the seat and watched Ben's strong-looking, bicep-bulging arms and big-fingered hands handle the rig with obvious expertise as he weaved them in and out of traffic at sixty and seventy miles per hour.

Little Oscar stared unabashedly at the stranger in his life, while Debbyanne smiled down at him and kissed the top of his blond, kinky-haired head.

Chapter 4

After Little Oscar finished his bottle of room-temperature-warm milk, Debbyanne finally got him to take his early afternoon nap by rubbing him gently on the back and repeating soft, cooing sounds. It was obvious he didn't like his new surroundings, fussing more than he ever had before. She couldn't fault him for it. The unfamiliar fifteen-by-fifteen-foot-square motel room had become a cell. They hadn't been outside its walls in three days, courtesy of Ben, the truck driver. The only contact they had with the outside world was the sounds of trucks and cars passing noisily by on the highway not far from the room. All Debbyanne knew was that they were on the outskirts of Capital City. But the motel room was adequate shelter for a brief stopover. Ben needed the time to get his rig repaired and serviced, before loading it with steel at the mill across the river, and returning north to Boston.

That was about as much information as she could get out of him. He wasn't interested in light conversa-

tion, or in serious communication, just sex in every way imaginable and as often as possible.

Debbyanne was thankful Little Oscar had accepted their temporary quarters, though only fitfully, getting him to sleep on the floor in a makeshift blanket bed. It kept him out of the way and off their bed, Ben's nightly sexual encounter center. Since he was paying for the room, and buying their food; take-out restaurant orders for her, supermarket baby food for Little Oscar, she did what he asked. And he asked a lot, from the moment they moved into the room. She used her body more in the last three days than over the past three years. If he left as planned that Wednesday evening, her debt to him would be paid in full. Of course, when alone again, she'd have the problem of finding a place to live in Capital City, a necessity with winter in the air.

Christmas was only five days off. She'd have to forget all about presents for them. Survival was at stake. But it galled her every time she thought about her parents not wanting her son living with them. So what if he was looking more colored like his father; and so what if any relatives visited over the holidays, and witnessed her disgrace in the flesh. That was their problem, not hers.

When she returned her thoughts to the present, she had to laugh inwardly at their motel scene. The close, warm, slightly fetid air smelled of Ben's body odor, her musky sex, and Little Oscar's pissy diapers soaking in the sink in the bathroom. And while she sat naked on the bed, Ben lay alongside her snoring airily through his long nose, and blowing air through his opened mouth. He was naked under the sheet and light wool blanket. Only Little Oscar was decent in his diaper and cotton shirt, lying asleep on his blanket floor bed next to the wall and wooden armchair.

Debbyanne reached down to touch herself between her legs and winced. Her private area was still sore

from the recent heavy traffic and sudden penetrations of Ben's celebrated twenty pounder. The ache in her rear end was also real from Ben's penchant for sexual novelty. "I like the old Hershey Bar route," he had announced the first night, brandishing a vaseline jar and daubing himself and her with the oily-smelling petroleum jelly.

Not to mention his need for oral gratification. He had readily admitted liking blow jobs even better than getting laid. Debbyanne had lost count, during their three-day sexual interlude, of just how many times she had fucked him, sucked him, or taken it up the rear end. For Ben, the male animal, who, she thought, was only masquerading as a human being, couldn't get enough sex every which way from her. She could only hope now in desperation that he would sleep through until it was time for him to go get his truck at six that evening.

But Debbyanne's luck didn't hold out.

A few minutes after three Ben woke up like the proverbial hungry bear in his den, stretching his hairy arms and grunting noisily. Debbyanne shooshed him to be quiet. Ben ignored her and continued his waking up ritual. When he finally did quiet down, he began ogling her nakedness, smiling thinly, barely showing any of his crooked front teeth. Then he resorted to playing with himself under the sheet and blanket. In only a minute he got a stiff-enough erection to show off. He poked Debbyanne on the shoulder bone with a blunt forefinger, and pointed down at the tent effect he had made of the covers.

"Guess what I got here, Deb, darling," Ben said, snickering in his dirty-sounding way, half nasal through his nose, half airy through his open mouth.

"I can see."

"Well, we gonna let him keep on standing tall? We're not gonna knock him down again?"

36

"Don't you ever get enough? My pussy's sore, and my ass still hurts."

"Nothing wrong with your mouth—is there?"

"That's the only part of me that isn't hurting."

"Well, come on then, darling, speak into this tube." Ben kicked off the sheet and blanket with his size eleven feet to reveal his seven-inch, purply-veined, erect penis in all its masculine splendor, though jutting in a slight curvature to the left and looking like an uncircumcised Cyclops sprouting from a black bushy-haired base.

"You're impossible, Ben. This is the last time. I've had it. You're not getting anymore after this."

"Okay, bitch, don't get bent out of shape. Just toot on it awhile, then I'll get dressed and go get my rig. And I promise, darling, I won't bother you no more." Then after a silent pause, with Debbyanne remaining where she sat on the bed, Ben added, "Aw, come on, Deb, darling, just suck on it a little bit for old Benny boy here—please!" When he reached over and caressed her bare back with his rough-skinned right hand, the palm and fingers feeling like sandpaper grating on her spinal column, she flinched.

Debbyanne made a face and slowly lowered her mouth over Ben's male hardness, while he sighed with obvious pleasure, a thin-lipped compressed smile beaming his satisfaction. As she became more orally active on it, he whispered husky-voiced endearments about how well she was doing on him, and offered steady encouragement, saying how she was going to make him come real soon.

But it was during Debbyanne's oral performance on Ben that Little Oscar woke up, rubbing his eyes and sitting up to look around the room for his mother. He had to crawl over to the bed and pull himself up its side to get a better view of her. And after watching his mother for some time, wide-eyed and silent, he started

to cry loud, aching sobs, his small flat chest heaving with each one.

Debbyanne quickly lifted her mouth off Ben's penis. "Oh, my God, Oscar's seen me blowing you!"

"So what? He don't know what you're doing. Get back down on it. I was just starting to come."

"Finish the job yourself."

"I can't blow myself, and jerking off is for kids."

"Then go find yourself a kid."

"You're a real smart ass, ain't you?"

Debbyanne didn't answer Ben. She slid off the bed and picked up Little Oscar, holding him close to her naked breasts, while he hugged her around the neck with his short arms, his tears wetting her shoulder. She patted him on the back. "Don't cry, honey, mommy's got you now."

But he didn't stop, shedding big baby tears that soaked her neck and shoulder, while he hugged her tightly around the neck.

"Shut the fucking kid up, and come on back here and finish what you started. My twenty pounder is dying from neglect. It's shriveling to a measly five pounder." Ben began pulling on his sagging member, while staring at Debbyanne with a pining, hurt expression around his deeply set dark eyes and craggy, Old Abe face.

Debbyanne didn't reply. She continued patting and rubbing Little Oscar's back, then got up and started pacing the worn, mottled green and rust carpeting alongside the bed.

Little Oscar only cried louder. His strangle hold almost choked off the air in Debbyanne's windpipe.

"If you can't get that kid to stop crying, maybe I can," Ben said with a sharp, harshly ominous edge to his voice, a distinct change from his softer, Southern drawl delivery. "Maybe a couple of slaps across his big

mouth'll make him quit yapping off, or maybe give him something to cry about for real."

"You touch my son, and I'll brain you."

"Hey, now don't you sound tough . . . and serious. Really makes my knees shake. I'm so scared, I just might shit myself."

"Try me."

"Just maybe I will." Ben hopped off the bed and sauntered around it on spindly legs, looking like a featherless rooster stalking a hen. His once proudly erect male stiffness sagged toward the floor like a short piece of meat.

Debbyanne backed up to the wall alongside the nightstand.

Ben smiled thinly and paused a second in front of her, then reached out quickly and grabbed her arms, shoulder high, as if playing two-handed touch football. "Gotcha!" he exclaimed, his lips parting widely to reveal silver fillings in his back molars. "Now gimme that kid." Ben pulled at Little Oscar, who screamed in his mother's ear, as he and Debbyanne tried to keep him from being taken out of her arms. When Ben stepped closer to Debbyanne, she lifted her knee solidly into his groin. He gasped, became wall-eyed like a rabbit, then moaned from deep in his throat. A grimace distorted his face. He released a screaming Little Oscar and collapsed to the carpeted floor, landing on his knees, quickly reaching cupped hands for his crotch. His head was level with Debbyanne's waist.

"You fucking bitch!" he hissed between clenched teeth and tightened lips. "I'll get your ass for this." He tried to get up, but sank back to his knees, moaning and crouching again before her.

"Like fuck you will," Debbyanne replied as she picked up a shaded ceramic lamp off the nearby nightstand next to her naked thigh and crashed it down on

Ben's dark-haired head with all of her thin-armed strength. It broke into halves, holding together by the inner electrical cord. Ben crumpled like a sack of loose potatoes to the carpeted floor at her feet. Debbyanne stepped over him. "We've got to get out of here fast— like right now," she said to her son, her voice a squeaky whisper. "So you stay here, honey," she added, placing Little Oscar on the bed. "Mommy has to get dressed." He stopped crying and sat quietly on the bed for her. "That's a good boy," Debbyanne said, brushing at his kinky hair. "Mommy would never let anybody hurt you. Not my precious baby. Not my honeybunch."

Debbyanne dressed herself and Little Oscar as if a woman on the run, and packed the overnight bag with equal alacrity, abandoning the wet diapers soaking in the bathroom. But before leaving the motel room, she rifled Ben's clothes on the wooden armchair, finding a bulging wallet in his trousers. She took out sixty-three dollars, leaving him his credit cards, and added the money to her parents' fifty-eight, and her own three, shoving the folded bills into her front right pocket. "Payment, Benny boy, for all the sucking and fucking you got out of me," she said, glancing over her shoulder at the unconscious truck driver lying on his back. Then she scooped up Little Oscar, the bag, and let herself out of the motel room. The chilled December air cooled her heated face and replaced the stale air in her lungs with the first full breath she took. But it looked gloomy. The sky was a solid gray overcast, ominously low with moisture, threatening to deposit the first snow of the coming winter season. She hurriedly buttoned the top button of her hand-me-down cloth coat and headed straight for the busy highway less than a hundred feet away.

She had already decided to try the older urban neighborhood where she had roomed with Little Oscar's father in a house owned by a Mrs. Addie James, a congenial, heavyset colored lady. Maybe the elderly Mrs.

James was still alive and renting rooms and apartments by the week.

She had enough money now to pay rent for awhile and to buy food. Later she'd see about getting a job, which would mean getting a baby-sitter for her son. But welfare would help her stay at home with him. The myriad possibilities ran through her mind as she hailed a slow-moving taxi and piled in the backseat, the bag beside her, Little Oscar on her lap. As the taxi left the curb and worked its way into the stream of traffic, she aimed a hurried glance toward the motel room and was relieved to see the door still closed and Ben nowhere in sight. She leaned back in the seat and said to the taxi driver, "Take us to the two-hundred block of Merry Street."

Debbyanne leaned her head back against the top of the seat and closed her eyes momentarily. What a relief it was to be free of that animal, Ben. She'd get quickly lost from him in the urban maze. Capital City had numerous narrow streets, just perfect for hiding from her past.

As for her future, she'd live one day at a time, and not try to plan too far ahead, complicating matters anymore than they were already in her soap opera life.

She opened her eyes and watched the parade of cars and trucks and buildings as the taxi moved swiftly toward their destination. It was going to be nice having her own place. The first thing she was going to do was to take a bath with water as hot as she could stand, to rid herself of Ben's stink. It would be like a new beginning for her body, once cleansed of its recent use by him. A sense of contentment settled over her.

Debbyanne hugged Little Oscar closer to her and could smell his unwashed hair. "I think we'd better take a bath together, honey," she whispered, "and won't that be fun." Little Oscar wiggled in her lap and waved his arms up and down. "Oh, I love you so much, my

little honeybunch," Debbyanne added, leaning her face against the side of her son's small head. She closed her eyes again and remained that way until she heard the taxi driver ask her for the exact address on Merry Street that she wanted to be let out. Debbyanne opened her eyes and recognized familiar buildings as they cruised slowly along the two-hundred block. It was like coming home for her. "Let us out here, driver," she replied, "I want to walk the rest of the way."

Chapter 5

The streetlights came on by the time Debbyanne arrived at the location where Mrs. Addie James used to live on Merry Street. The charred remains of the three-story frame apartment building looked like scattered, partially buried blackened corpses sticking up at odd angles out of the mound of dirt and debris that filled the exposed cellar.

Debbyanne stood rigidly, as if her desert boots were glued to the concrete sidewalk, staring at the emptiness. A cold sadness engulfed her like a shroud. She'd grown fond of that old house. Little Oscar had been created inside her in the rear third-floor efficiency apartment that had looked out on the treeless backyard. It had always been hot in the summer and inadequately heated during winter, a dingy setting for a young couple. But it had been the only place where Debbyanne had ever experienced acceptance and love, desired and appreciated just for herself. And it had been hers to do

with as she pleased, a liberty she never had in her parents' farmhouse.

Little Oscar's father had always made her feel important to him and needed. The dismal furnishings and the peeling wallpaper had meant nothing to her. It was the exchange of feelings, the total, mutual sharing of a life together that counted. Now even those sweet memories were shattered like glass with the destruction of Mrs. Addie James' building.

Her son's weight suddenly became leaden, while the air grew colder. A gust of wind swept scraps of loose newspaper across her scuffed, ankle-high boots and brushed against the bottoms of her faded hip-hugger jeans. She picked up the heavy, bulging overnight bag and started walking again. To where? She wasn't sure this time, but she had to keep moving—or die inside. She fought back tears and hoped the walking would get her warm again.

Three long city blocks from Mrs. Addie James' former apartment building location, Debbyanne came to the bus terminal and quickly decided to retreat from the unfriendly weather outdoors and rest inside its warmer restaurant. There she could get something to eat and feed Little Oscar his baby food, before making a final decision, whether to stay in Capital City or to go somewhere else. Where? Again she had no idea.

Debbyanne sat in a booth and fed Little Oscar the last of his strained spinach, carrots and applesauce, before eating her California burger, French fries and coleslaw. She didn't realize how hungry she was, until she started eating. She gave Little Oscar a long, crispy, brown French fry to keep him occupied while she ate. Afterwards, she relaxed quietly over a cup of hot coffee.

And in a short time, she almost forgot where she was. Little Oscar became a distant blur sitting nearby

in the highchair provided by the waitress as her thoughts lingered on their situation. She tried to visualize their heading somewhere else, such as Florida, remembering pictures in school geography books and encyclopedias and posters in travel bureau window displays depicting sand, surf and palm trees swaying in tropical breezes. They wouldn't freeze to death there as they would in Capital City, if they didn't get a place to live—and soon—before winter arrived full tilt with its icy blasts. A hotel for the night would suit them temporarily, but she'd have to look for a permanent place to live, starting early in the morning. Maybe she'd stop by a couple of real estate offices in town, or check the classified ads in the newspapers. She nodded unconsciously at her random thoughts, while staring blankly at the yellow vinyl booth seat across from her, chin resting on her left closed fist, her right hand holding the coffee cup.

Her muse was broken when a tall black man stopped alongside Little Oscar's highchair and stared down at her, a wide smile spreading across his wide-cheeked, angular face. He was spectacularly dressed in a fawn-colored, wide-brimmed hat, matching open topcoat and wide-lapelled suit, plus wide-width tie. The only article of clothing different in color was his dark brown shirt. A sparkling diamond tie pin glittered for her attention, competing with a sapphire ring on his left hand and an emerald ring on his right hand. He was colorful, to say the least. His teeth were a contrasting white surrounded by his dark-skinned face. His continuing smile was infectious. All Debbyanne could do was smile back at him.

"You're looking down, baby."

His voice was deep, raspy resonant, and strongly masculine.

Debbyanne nodded agreement, but didn't reply.

"Couldn't help but notice you and your kid, 'cause he looks like his daddy was a soul brother."

"He was."

"Then you won't mind if I join you?" The tall black man slid gracefully into the empty booth seat across from her. "I'm Lonny McCall." He smiled again, only wider.

Debbyanne noticed he had a gold tooth on the left side of his mouth.

Little Oscar's small round face contorted into a frightened grimace. He reached his short arms out to his mother.

Debbyanne recognized the sign. Little Oscar was about to cry because of the sudden intrusion. She lifted him out of the highchair and sat him on her lap, while reassuring him that it was all right to have this man sit near them.

When Little Oscar was settled, she replied, "I'm Debbyanne and this is Oscar." She took a deep breath and could smell Lonny's heady, sweet after shave and cologne, wondering if he had used the entire contents of each bottle that night. And besides smelling good, everything about him was clean and shiny, including his manicured fingernails.

After a smiling pause, with the side gold tooth glinting in the overhead lighting, Lonny said, "I got some time to kill, and you look like you got troubles, little momma. I can see it in your face. You look worried around your eyes. Want to tell me your problems? Maybe I can help."

"You're very observing, Lonny. I do have one big problem. I need a place to stay tonight, then get something permanent. I went to see if Mrs. James still had her apartment building on Merry Street, where I used to live, and found nothing but an empty lot. Must've burned down recently. Now I'm stuck for a place to live, till I can start supporting myself and my son."

"Oh, yeah, Addie James, the heavyset, property-owning woman. Her place got burned down this past summer, during the riots. But her building wasn't the only one. This whole town looked like a torch parade. Never seen so many fires at the same time. A lot of pyros got their jollies watching the flames. All the streets around here got messed up. Store windows got busted. Cars got overturned. A real bad scene. The cop pigs shot target practice on the looting brothers and sisters."

"I thought it was strange. So many buildings looked damaged and boarded up. And vacant lots where I'd remembered houses had been, when I left a year ago."

"Yeah, it was a bad scene. Lots of hate on both sides of the racial line." After a smiling pause, Lonny added, "But tough Lonny can solve your problem, just like that." He snapped his long, shiny-skinned black thumb and forefinger, their manicured nails brilliant with clear polish under the overhead lighting.

"How?"

"You can stay with me, until you get your own apartment."

"That's very nice of you, but . . ."

"Is his daddy around for support?" Lonny nodded toward Little Oscar.

"No, he's dead."

"O-deed on drugs? Got shot by the cop pigs?"

"No, a street fight."

Lonny nodded again, his wide-brimmed hat looking like a fancy round sail on his head. "You can get welfare with a kid."

"I know."

"Your social worker'll help you find an apartment."

"I guess that might be the answer for awhile. But I'd rather support myself."

"You can collect welfare and work part-time on the side."

"With a baby to take care of?"

"The kid's no problem while he's small. You can turn some tricks right at home. There's good money in it."

"Oh, I don't know if I could do it with just anybody and everybody."

"You've been giving your pussy away for nothing—right? Why not make some money doing it from now on?"

"You've got a point there."

"I can set you up in style with some nice rags. Get you some high-class dudes for clients. No trash. Even get a steady baby-sitter, if you got to go out to meet your date." Lonny paused and looked at Little Oscar, who was sucking on another French fry Debbyanne had given him.

"I'll think about it," she replied, brushing at her son's hair.

"You do that little momma. But in the meantime, you need a place to sleep—tonight. And it's getting colder outside by the minute. Winter's just around the corner, and coming on fast."

"I know."

"You're invited to stay at my place tonight."

After a pause, while Debbyanne looked at her son, then at the smiling black stranger across from her, and finally glancing at the forbidding darkness outside through the restaurant's large, street-fronting windows, she replied, "All right, Lonny, I'll take a chance and go with you. But I'm touchy about one thing. I don't do anything obscene while he's awake. It makes me feel cheap and funny inside, if my son sees me doing something with a man I shouldn't be doing, even if he can't understand what I'm doing.

"I can dig it, little momma. Now come on, I'll pay for your eats here. We've got to get your kid in bed. Looks like he's falling asleep already."

"He is. We've been a couple of gypsies these last few days. I feel so bad for him. He's such a good boy. And I could use some sleep myself—after a nice hot bath. I feel crummy."

"Everything's going to be just fine, little momma, because you're in Lonny's hands. And nobody hurts when I'm in charge. I'm a one-man charity board. First, we'll get you settled tonight, then tomorrow morning I'll get one of my girls to take you downtown to the welfare people. And take the kid. They'll want to see him. And once you're settled in your own place, we can arrange for you to make some good part-time money turning a trick or two, without those nosy welfare people finding out. You'll be able to live good and take care of your kid like you should. And I always guarantee happy endings, when I'm looking after things." Lonny released one of his big, white smiles with a hint of gold.

"I hope you're right."

"You just follow my lead, little momma."

Lonny escorted Debbyanne and Little Oscar out of the restaurant to the nearby parking lot and opened the door to a long, metallic-silver Cadillac. Debbyanne had never been inside such a luxurious car. But she settled comfortably onto the black velour front seat alongside Lonny with Little Oscar on her lap and the overnight bag between her legs on the floor under the dashboard.

It was a fairly long ride through the inner city streets from the bus terminal, before they parked in front of a four-story brick apartment building in another part of the city, a section she'd never seen before, with its naked-limbed trees lining the wider streets that were clean and free of debris. The other buildings were also undamaged and well-maintained.

Across the street the city's largest park spread out as far as she could see in the streetlamp-lit night. She'd heard about the park, but never visited it. Debbyanne

made a mental note to take Little Oscar there soon to see the animals in the zoo compound. It would be like having a touch of the country nearby. The open spaces were a lure. She was still a farmgirl at heart.

Debbyanne liked Lonny's second-floor apartment. Each room had a different color motif. The living room had subdued shades of gold. The dining room featured ebony furniture and stark white walls. The kitchen was yellow bright with modern wood cabinets and every gadget and appliance built-in, while the master bedroom was done in pleasant greens. The bathroom had speckled brown and tan carpeting that climbed the walls to the textured white ceiling. Its only tile was in the shower stall. The guest bedroom was done in soft blues. And after bathing Little Oscar, Debbyanne put him to sleep on its single bed, protecting him with pillows and chairs from the kitchen to make sure he didn't fall off.

Once he was safely out of the way and sleeping, Debbyanne took a hot soaking bath and shampooed her long blonde hair. Later, she joined Lonny in his bedroom, sitting with him on the green and white floral print love seat. She was dressed in his blue, half-sleeve kimono, he in a wine-red lounging robe over matching pajamas and fluffy slippers. Her feet were bare like the rest of her body inside the kimono. The room smelled of burning punk.

"Try this good Moroccan hash for a starter, baby," Lonny said, "it'll help get you up to a groovy high." He took a drag off the cigarette with the antique white paper. "It's the best money can buy. Got a stronger kick than regular grass."

Debbyanne and Lonny took *hits* off the joint until it was too small to hold with their fingertips and Lonny used a silver *roach* holder to get the last puffs out of the acrid, punky-smelling butt. Then he opened a small

bottle of chilled Mateus Rose. The wine tasted fruity and cool on her tongue. And with the alcohol working its way quickly into her bloodstream, after the *hash* smoke had wormed its way up into her brain, she felt mellow and totally relaxed, almost limp, free-floating, as if hovering above them rather than sitting.

When the bottle was empty, Lonny took her by the hand, his large and black, hers small and pink-white. He led her to the round bed without a headboard. She let him lay her full-length on its pale green velvet bedspread over the soft, giving mattress. The sensation of spinning on a merry-go-round overwhelmed her. She closed her eyes and waited for him to undress. Already naked under her borrowed robe, she spread her legs and arms and abandoned herself to the luxury of the bed.

Lonny studied her pale pink-white body a moment after he joined her on the bed. "You are one fine-looking white fox, little momma," he said in his deeply masculine raspy voice as he caressed and stroked her pliant, smooth skin from her neck downward over sloping breasts and flattened stomach, then finger-probed her navel. He also stroked the inside flesh of her thighs and gently brushed his fingertips against her pubic hair at the confluence of her sleek legs. Lastly, he worked his long middle finger into her moist vagina. "I just have to touch you all over, baby, before I put my big black monster into your pretty pink pussy."

Debbyanne lay still and enjoyed the swirling inner warmth, while the sensitivity of her skin's nerve endings vibrated at his light touch. The merry-go-round effect was still with her. Her brain was filled with spinning cells. She was weightless and miles above them, yet anchored to the luxurious bed where she let Lonny do anything he wanted to her, finger-probing, hand-caressing and lip-kissing her shimmering flesh.

When Lonny lay full-length on top of her, feeling his total weight, and his large male member enter her eas-

ily, opening up to him like a spreading umbrella from his masculine force, Debbyanne moaned from the sensation.

To her surprise, it didn't hurt; as when that animal, Ben, the truck driver, had shoved his big thing up inside her so many times.

"Oh, Lonny, it feels so good," Debbyanne said with a voice that sounded disjointed from her throat, as if it came out of a loudspeaker somewhere else in the darkened bedroom. "And it's so nice here with you, I never want to wake up. Never."

"Yeah, ain't it a groove, baby?"

"Yes, Lonny, it's a groove."

PART II

Chapter 1

It was lunchtime and Little Oscar had spent most of the brisk sunny October Saturday morning outdoors with the other neighborhood kids riding skateboards on the sidewalks and street, dodging cars and trucks. He loved his new fiberglass model. It was light and fast. He won more races with it than he lost. And he was becoming expert at keeping his balance on it, seldom falling off.

When he finally retreated indoors, he stored his skateboard in a cardboard box in the living room coat closet near the hallway door to their fourth-floor apartment. They had been living there three years, after moving out of a cramped three small rooms in a different section of Capital City, which had been home ever since he could remember. He liked this apartment better, having a bedroom of his own. It meant he didn't have to sleep on the sofa in the living room when some man stayed overnight with his mother. He hated that. Little Oscar liked sleeping with his mother himself.

She was soft and warm and always hugging him close to her, even when she was asleep. She was the only big person he liked or trusted. His mother never went back on her word, and was always nice to him. She never made him do chores he hated. He did what he liked to do when he felt like doing it. And she always got him toys to play with after he saw them advertised on TV.

As for the other big people in his life, from the different social workers checking up on them all the time, to his teachers in the various elementary schools he had attended, and the men who came around to the apartment, with some staying longer than others, he never liked or trusted any of them. Little Oscar sensed that none of the men wanted him around, or liked him, either. Because when he was there, his mother wouldn't let them fool around with her, pawing at her breasts, and rubbing on her legs, or pushing their hard crotches against her. But they were cardboard people to him. He had his mother. She was the only one who mattered to him. He even wished he could grow up fast and marry his mother, keeping her all to himself, and away from those men, who looked like giants to him. He hated looking up at them all the time. It hurt his neck and made him feel small, smaller than he actually was.

Sometimes his mother talked to him about his dead father. How nice he had been to her. Better than the others. But still Little Oscar could never picture his father inside his head, like seeing a movie or watching television, even when his mother described him in detail. His father never existed in person to him, but his mother always *was,* always existed for him. All he cared about was being with her and staying as happy as he was with her now, especially when he didn't have to share her with men, which, to his dismay, wasn't too often.

When his mother talked about her parents, she always got a mad-eyed, drumskin-tight look on her face.

And her voice got a hard sound to it each time she repeated the story about how her father wanted her to give him up when he was a baby. How she ran away again in order to keep him all to herself, and how she loved him so much. Said her folks were mean to her and had no heart or feelings, like normal parents. They never did anything nice for her the way they did for her older brothers and sisters. Said she came along too late. They didn't want to be bothered raising her. Yet they had fussed over the others. They were older and were tired of responsibility. She was an unwanted burden to them.

His mother hated her people. And he got to dislike them almost as much, even though he had only a fuzzy picture of them in his head as to what they actually looked like from what his mother said, describing them in detail.

But she did talk nice about the farm and the animals. How she had raised her own kid goat that its mother wouldn't nurse, and her father didn't want to bother saving. How she had loved the scenery, the rolling hills, the spread of cornfields, the vegetable garden and the woods surrounding the farm. She'd go exploring in the back where the creek crossed the property. And how she loved the fresh clean air. A lot nicer and better to breathe than the factory- and traffic-polluted air in Capital City. It was a lot quieter, too. No cars, trucks or buses rumbling by all night. No street people hollering and fighting in the overcrowded neighborhoods. All this talk by his mother about the farm stirred vague yearnings to go see this place for himself. Maybe live on it someday and meet these people who were supposed to be relatives.

When he didn't find his mother in the apartment at lunchtime, Little Oscar guessed that she had gone to either the nearby corner grocery store, to the liquor

store or downstairs to talk and drink coffee with fat Mrs. Meyers. So he made a peanut butter and grape jelly sandwich on white bread and got a can of grape soda from the refrigerator, then sat at the kitchen table. A pile of food-stained dishes from last night's supper was still in the sink unwashed. Little Oscar ate the thickly sliced tasty sandwich and sipped the sweet, cold soda in silence, waiting for his mother to come home. But he soon wondered where her current boyfriend was, since Little Oscar didn't like him and was uncomfortable in his company, while aware the boyfriend didn't like him in return. They kept a wary distance from each other.

And wasn't this current boyfriend of hers the craziest man he ever met. Always doing practical jokes around the apartment, hiding things on his mother, setting booby traps to make things fall on her when she opened a closet door, plus inviting his crazy friends up to sponge meals off his mother, drink her liquor, laugh and talk to the wee small hours of the morning, smoking their stinky dope that stunk up the place. Little Oscar hated those long, noisy nights. And didn't that crazy dude like to bait the cops into arresting him when he was high on dope, or dizzy on booze. No wonder his nickname was Loco. His real name was Wayne Byrd, but Loco fitted him better. He was like a big silly kid, instead of a grown, serious man. Yet he was never friendly or playful with Little Oscar, and never gave him any encouragement to be friendly back and do things together, either.

Little Oscar decided some time ago that he'd like it much better around the apartment if he could get rid of Loco. He secretly hoped his mother would get into a big fight with the wild man and kick him out of their place. She had said often enough that she was fed up with his lies, saying how he was looking for work, when he was just goofing around. Loco never did help too long with

paying bills, or with buying food, since the welfare money never made it to the end of the month, as he had promised when he moved in permanently with his backpack and guitar. And didn't that fool quit his job last week. Never did last more'n a month on any job. Always something was happening to make him quit or get fired. And wasn't his mother still mad at Loco for quitting his latest job. She hardly spoke to him all week. He wished his mother would dump the sucker.

Little Oscar amused himself while he ate the last of the sandwich and drank the remaining ounce of grape soda thinking about ways to get rid of Loco. When finished, he wandered into the living room, then headed toward his bedroom, which was next to his mother's, looking for something interesting to do to pass the time until his mother got back. But when he stopped a moment at her bedroom door and heard stirring inside, someone moving things around, it raised his curiosity a notch. He peeked through the crack of space between the back edge of the door and the jamb and saw Loco hunched over the bureau, rifling through his mother's pocketbook, then take money out of her wallet and stuff it into the front right pocket of his raggedy, patched jeans.

Little Oscar didn't wait to see anymore, tiptoeing quickly out of the apartment. He ran down the three flights of stairs and was pounding on Mrs. Meyers' door in less than a minute. *I'm gonna tell Mom. She'll kick his dirty butt out for sure now.* A crescent-shaped grin spread from ear to ear at the prospect. He kept pounding on the wooden door till his small fist hurt.

Mrs. Meyers had barely opened the door, when Little Oscar shouted, "Hey, Mom," brushing past the fat older woman with the dyed red hair, running into the kitchen where he knew his mother would be, adding, "Loco's stealing money outta your pocketbook."

Debbyanne banged the coffee cup down on its matching saucer. "That son-of-a-bitch! I better go stop him before he rips off all my money. Thanks for the coffee, Blanche."

"Men, you can't trust none of 'em. Believe me, I know," Blanche Meyers shouted after Debbyanne and Little Oscar as they stampeded out of the apartment.

Little Oscar led his mother back up the three flights of stairs, hopping two at a time. But at their apartment, he waited for his mother to go in first, trailing her into the bedroom where Loco was on the phone, his back to the door. "Don't sweat it, turkey. I got the bread. I want the best Panama Red you got. I'll be down to get it tonight pronto, man."

"You've got the money all right—mine—you fucking thief!" Debbyanne screamed at Loco, just as he hung up the receiver. When Loco turned around, a wide-eyed expression on his auburn-bearded face, he looked like a guilty schoolboy. "Whataya talking about?" His voice was whiny.

"My son saw you taking money out of my pocketbook. So don't try to bullshit your way out of it."

"That little nigger fink."

"You pack your gear and take a hike. And don't call my son names again. And make sure you take your stupid guitar with you. I'm fed up with carrying your ass, and listening to your lousy singing and playing. I'm having enough problems supporting myself and my son. I don't need a deadbeat around here to hassle me—or to steal off me."

"Aw, come on, Deb, I only took a couple-three bucks. I wanta buy some grass. I could use a good high. I've been depressed lately."

"You're a bum, you know that? I should have my head examined, letting you sponge off me this long."

"What's the problem? I'll pay my own way, soon's I get another job. Give me some time, huh?"

"You're a stupid fucking idiot for quitting your job, you know that?"

"Aw, Deb, I couldn't hack the bullshit. I hate factory work. I'll get a job in construction. It's healthier working outdoors."

"And in the meantime you eat my food, drink my booze, pop my pills and sleep in my bed, then have the nerve to steal my money when I'm not around."

"Cool it, huh, Deb? Here's your fucking money." Loco pulled out a fistful of bills and tossed the squashed paper money at Debbyanne. Lumplike, it dropped quickly to the carpeted floor in front of her. "I'm going back to bed. All this haggling's made me tired and depressed again." The scrunched up bills lay in a pile on the purple nylon carpet.

"You're a lazy fuck, you know that?"

"It runs in my family." Loco dropped heavily onto the double bed, its inner springs squeaking in protest. He folded his hands behind his head on the pillow.

"At least take your dirty sneakers off, ingrate."

"You never make the bed, why sweat my sneakers?"

"I want your lazy ass out of here by the time I come back tonight. And I mean out—packed and gone."

"Up yours," Loco replied, giving Debbyanne the middle finger sign. "I'll leave when I'm good and ready. Now buzz off, I wanta blow some zeeze again."

"We're through, you goddamn idiot. We've been through a long time. Can't you get the hint?"

"No way I'm leaving. I like it here."

"I guess I'm going to have to dynamite your ass out." Debbyanne head-motioned Little Oscar to follow her out of the bedroom. In the kitchen she made herself a cup of instant coffee. Little Oscar sat across the kitchen table drinking another can of grape soda, his gaze glued on his mother.

"You want him out of here, right, Mom?"

"Oh, God, yes, honey. He's overstayed his welcome.

I'm sick of his stupid practical jokes, which he thinks are so funny, and I can't stand his smelly socks. And everytime he kisses me with that scratchy beard of his, I could scream. He's a leftover hippie from the sixties, with his beat-up guitar and scroungy backpack."

"What's a hippie, Mom?"

"A dirty bum who won't work."

"That sure sounds like Loco."

"Doesn't it? Oh, God, how I'd like to get him to take a hike, permanently. He's obnoxious. I can't stand to sleep in the same bed with him anymore. He stinks."

"Betcha you'd rather have me sleep with you, right, Mom?"

"Sure, honey, you're mommy's lover."

"I love you more'n anybody else in the whole world, Mom."

"And I love you, too. More than anything and everything. You were a part of me once. I can never forget that."

"I'm gonna get rid of Loco for you, Mom."

"How can a little boy like you do that?"

"Don't know yet, Mom, but I'll think of something."

"In the meantime, I'll have to cruise the bars tonight and hustle some money to get us through next week. I thought I was finished with that kind of life, when big talker Loco promised to be my sponsor, if I let him move in here with us and I was his faithful girl friend. What a fool I was to believe that lying jerk. I even hoped I could get off welfare, and not have to put up with snooping social workers once a month. God, how I hate those women sticking their noses in my business."

"I don't like it when Loco sleeps with you."

"I know that, honey, but I need a good man for protection, and to make me feel like a woman."

"But you got me, Mom, and that Loco is no good for you."

"I know. And I'm really happy I've got you for a son."

"If I get rid of Loco for you, Mom, will you let me sleep with you again . . . and you'll play with me again?"

"Oh, you're really something, my little honeybunch."

Little Oscar giggled and looked up at his mother from under his blond eyebrows, his head tilted forward slightly. Then his mother patted his face gently, and they exchanged knowing grins.

Little Oscar waited in his bedroom that night until he heard Loco moving around in his mother's bedroom. Having observed the man's habits for a long time, more months than he could remember, Little Oscar figured Loco would leave about eleven, with his mother already out trying to make money for them to buy food during the following week, since the welfare money had already been spent for October. When Loco was by himself, he never stayed all night in the apartment. He was too fidgety to lie around and watch television. Little Oscar knew he had a thirst for a *high*. He'd go get his dope as he said he would on the phone earlier.

But before he left the apartment, Loco went into the kitchen and drank an entire six-pack of beer. He amused and entertained himself, laughing and cackling and belching.

Little Oscar used the opportunity to get his skateboard and slip out of the apartment unnoticed by Loco. He walked with careful steps down the stairs to the third-floor landing, where he placed the skateboard on the second step down at a twenty degree angle toward the leading edge of the riser. It was out of the range of the hall's weak ceiling light, which left the steps in shadowy light, if any at all. Little Oscar calculated Loco would do the rest for him.

He snickered to himself and climbed the stairs again, stepping on the front part of his stockinged feet, keeping his heels off the rubber tread covers, making as little sound as possible.

Loco never checked up on him when they were alone in the apartment before, so Little Oscar was confident he wouldn't that night. He didn't go back to the apartment, instead retreated to the darker end of the fourth-floor hallway and stood in the door entrance of the vacant apartment adjacent to theirs. The tenants had moved out only last week. It was a perfect place to wait.

A short time later, as expected, Loco shuffled out of the apartment, leaving the door ajar, and headed toward the stairs.

Little Oscar listened to his clumsy tripping down the first flight of stairs, and again to his toe-scraping shuffle on the landing. Holding his breath, Little Oscar could hear his own pulse beat in his ears. It would be an unscheduled flight for Loco down those stairs. And it came on schedule, as Little Oscar planned it that night.

"Whaa—agghh," was all Little Oscar could make out, followed by thumping and bumping, then total silence, after the expected sudden dead stop at the bottom of those steep, narrow stairs.

The skateboard made its own abrupt banging sounds in accompanying Loco's body noises. Little Oscar found it halfway down the stairs upside down with its wheels still spinning. But he didn't go all the way down to look at Loco, to see if he was still breathing. He just glanced a second at the still form in the landing's semidarkness. Then he retrieved his skateboard and ran back upstairs on stocking feet, dressed in his pajamas.

By the time he was inside the apartment, standing near the open door, he heard voices floating upstairs, and assumed Loco had been discovered by the downstairs tenants. His heart was still beating hard inside

his airtight chest. He put his skateboard back into the closet and retreated to his bedroom, where he stood by the window looking down on the street. He opened the window to hear better. The cold air teased his warm face. He waited for the ambulance that was sure to arrive. Loco couldn't have gotten up after that long, steep fall. He must've landed smack on his head, the way he was lying there in a heap, feet and legs propped up against the wall, looking like a loose-jointed rag doll with not a bone in its body.

Then like clockwork, only minutes later, a siren-blaring ambulance speeded up to their apartment building. Its flashing roof lights rotated crimson beams of light outward into the street's lamp-lit semidarkness like a revolving horizontal fan.

Later, when the attendants carried Loco out on a stretcher, the white cover was only up to his neck, with his face exposed. He was still alive. Little Oscar watched the ambulance take Loco away toward the hospital on the far side of town, its roof lights flashing again and its siren blaring a warning to the other vehicles in its way. But it wasn't long before its wail and lights were lost to his senses, disappearing into the night as quickly as it came.

Little Oscar couldn't sleep after that. He could only lie on his bed and stare at the shadows on the ceiling, waiting for his mother to come home. As soon as he heard his mother's heavy, obviously tired tread up the stairs in the early hours of Sunday morning, he jumped off his bed and ran to greet her at the living room door with the news.

"Mom, Mom, Loco fell down the stairs. Must've broke his neck and busted up his head real bad. The ambulance came and took him to the hospital."

When the wide-eyed shock had dissipated from her tired face and she had gasped for air from behind a

hand held over her lips, Debbyanne asked her son, "How did he do that? Was he drunk, or stoned?"

"I don't know, Mom, honest," Little Oscar replied, looking up at his mother from under lowered blond eyebrows and tilted head.

"You sure, honey?"

"Uh huh," Little Oscar said, squirming and shifting his weight from one foot to the other. "Loco drank the six-pack you bought yesterday. Maybe he was drunk and tripped. Them stairs is steep."

"I guess I better call the hospital and . . ."

"Why, Mom?" Litte Oscar asked his mother. "He wasn't my daddy. And he ain't your husband. We don't need him around here anymore—right?"

"You're right, honey. He's nothing to me . . . really. But when the cops come checking on the accident and start asking a lot of questions, we'll just tell them he was visiting here for awhile, until he got his own place. And that he came and went whenever he pleased. And that he was a heavy drinker and smoked grass and popped pills, a real junkhead. They'll know all about his busts. He's got an arrest record a mile long. So who'll care about him on the police force? He's probably garbage in their eyes. Besides, we're not legally responsible for his smelly ass. We're not his blood relatives. Let the cops find out if he's got any people, if he has to stay in the hospital and runs up a big bill. I've paid enough of his goddamn debts."

"Suppose he dies, Mom?"

"Then we'll let his relatives bury the drunken pothead. He wasn't my husband—right? Nothing but a lazy, overaged hippie bum. I should have my head examined for getting involved with a guy like him. Only Lonny had any class. I miss Lonny. Haven't seen him in years. I wonder if he's still in jail?"

"You don't need nobody but me, Mom. I'll take good care of you when I grow up, 'cause I love you more than

felt happy and secure beside the one he loved—his mom.

Late Sunday afternoon a pair of young policemen
finally arrived at their apartment building and began
the investigation of the accident. They had already re-
viewed Loco's arrest record of drug and drunk busts, so
conducted the tenant interviews with routine, obviously minimum interest. In their outspoken opinion,
Loco was just another of the garbage-type street people
they dealt with daily. They were just going through the
motions of an investigation for the record.

So they readily accepted Debbyanne and Little Oscar's descriptions of Loco's drinking and dope habits,
and their explanations that Loco was probably high on
beer and grass, having drunk an entire six-pack before
he left, and who knows what else he drank or smoked.
Also that he most likely tripped over his own uncoor-
dinated feet on the dark, poorly lighted stairs with
their torn carpeting. Because all he cared about was
getting high, having laughs, and playing practical jokes
on people.

Besides, they weren't relatives, so they weren't liable for him. He was just staying temporarily in her
apartment, nothing permanent or legal about their relationship, therefore Debbyanne wouldn't assume any
responsibility for his hospital bills, or other costs, if he
didn't pull through.

The policemen nodded their heads in agreement
with her and said that they understood, then left, leaving behind a relieved Debbyanne and Little Oscar, who
exchanged knowing grins in smug silence as they listened to the fading footsteps down the stairs.

When Loco died that Sunday evening, having never
regained consciousness, a prompt autopsy by the hospital pathologist revealed a higher-than-average content

of alcohol in his blood, which corroborated Debbyanne and Little Oscar's capsule explanation of the cause of the accident: a semidrunken condition and lack of coordination, since Loco was no athlete and never one for grace and balance. It satisfied the police authorities. They promptly buried the case in their closed files section.

Loco himself was buried in a potter's field grave, with no one from his past life attending. The city welfare people paid the hospital bills and the funeral costs. And his pallbearers were paid professionals supplied by the hired undertaker, since no relatives could be found locally, nor did any of his cronies express any interest in a dead Loco.

Debbyanne had turned over his meager belongings to the police: a pair of greasy, dirty jeans, a couple of old army fatigue shirts that smelled of his acrid body odor, worn sandals, two pairs of odorous sneakers, a nicked wooden guitar with a broken string and his backpack with the missing strap, gladly releasing them in case any relatives did eventually show up to claim his worldly possessions.

So while they lowered Loco's body into the ground of a suburban cemetery that following Saturday, a week after the accident, Debbyanne and Little Oscar remained at home and chatted quietly about the weather over cups of warm cocoa topped with melting marshmallows, since it had turned chilly and rainy in the afternoon. It was too damp and dismal a day to be outside, even more depressing to be burying a nonperson like Loco.

Later that same day, when Debbyanne found a pair of his old, stiff, rank socks under the bed in her bedroom, she promptly threw them into the garbage can kept in the cabinet under the kitchen sink. It would be put out for garbage collection on Monday with the rest of the trash. She liked the idea. It would be ridding

herself completely of any and all tangible reminders of Loco.

Little Oscar volunteered to take the garbage down for collection on Monday morning, when he left for school. It would be a first for him.

Chapter 2

Six months after Loco's fall into death, leaving Debbyanne without a man to sustain her physically and
socially, as well as sharing in the financial burden of
supplementing their subsistence-level welfare income,
she decided to change her luck and move to another
part of the city.

Besides, she hated the lingering glances from the
other tenants in the building, those lengthy, wide-eyed,
eyebrow-lifting stares. Yet none of them ever broached
the subject, asking her what happened that night with
Loco. But she still didn't like their silent questioning
treatment. Even Blanche Meyers got funny about it,
hinting at the possibility that everything wasn't kosher
about the fall, since the Wilsons, a black couple who
lived on the second floor, had mentioned hearing footsteps running up the stairs afterwards. The Wilsons
never told the police about it during the inquiry, since
street people never tell the cop pigs anything, especially
black street people. The sooner the police completed

71

their investigation, the sooner they'd leave, giving the building back to its occupants. Nobody in his right mind wanted them snooping around the place any longer than necessary.

But the unspoken mental probes of doubt provided Debbyanne with sufficient motivation to move. And she readily admitted it to herself. Money matters and the absence of male company were only surface rationale to explain the sudden change of residence during the month of April the following year.

They moved to a smaller three rooms on the second floor of an aged clapboard and brick single-family house that had been converted to a two-family residence with an apartment on each floor. It was less than spacious, and not as well-lighted as the apartment they had left.

Since Debbyanne had the only bedroom, Little Oscar slept on the divan bed in the living room, which doubled as his bedroom at night. The kitchen's only window looked out on the rear alley, its concrete paving continually strewn with broken glass and house garbage. The downstairs apartment had the use of the postage stamp-size yard.

Little Oscar didn't like the kids in his new neighborhood. He had fights with them daily, protecting his possessions, or when he preferred walking on the sidewalk instead of in the street as ordered by some bully in front of the kid's house. Getting his skateboard back after someone borrowed it, or when older kids tried to ride it home and keep it, proved difficult, making it necessary for his mother to intervene. He soon became a target.

So Little Oscar started staying indoors more that spring and summer, watching TV after school let out, having more blocks of unused time to fill than he knew how to when the daylight hours lengthened. For Little Oscar the long hot summer days had thirty hours rather than twenty-four. The wise, tough, pushy neigh-

borhood punks surrounded his building like an army of ants, and he virtually became a prisoner in the apartment at times, afraid to go outdoors to seek new friends. He wasn't as strong as most of the others his age, and the big older kids were always a menace to him.

The bedroom-living room combination had been acceptable to Little Oscar up until his mother got another boyfriend, which resulted in a quick loss of privacy for him when this stranger named Buck barged into their lives. Buck was the only name he and his mother knew the man by, since he wouldn't tell anybody his real name. He said people always laughed at it.

Buck was a big man, big enough to be a tight end in pro football, and liked to work out with weights in a local gym to maintain his bigness. He had arms as thick as ten pound hams, with bulging shoulder and chest muscles to match. And he always wore sleeveless tank shirts or black leather vests over a bare-skinned upper torso, which displayed his rippling muscular physique to advantage when the weather was warm. If it got chilly at night, or during colder weather, Buck wore tight-fitting turtleneck shirts tucked into his pants, which emphasized his slim twenty-nine-inch waist in contrast with his broad shoulders and chest. He said it turned women on, and he liked to turn women on.

Buck's head was leonine, with his crown of curly black hair always in massive disarray. His face was as wide as a phone book, and his big nose stuck out like a loaf of Italian crust bread. Black hairs protruded from the oval nostrils. Even his big ears had black hairs sticking out of them like wild weeds. Only his size nine feet were diminutive in comparison to his six-five frame, which caused him to walk with a forward pitch, as if always having trouble keeping his balance. But nobody looked at Buck's feet. His cold blue eyes and

bulk attracted attention to his broad-featured face, out of fear mostly, since he exuded a primitive aura, with a hint of total belligerency, plus a passion for violence.

Yet Debbyanne never experienced fear of the dangerous animal in Buck. Instead she saw a man strong enough to fill her womanly needs. After a few dates, Buck became her new sponsor. And since he had his own one-room efficiency apartment three blocks away on an intersecting side street with the wider main thoroughfare they lived on, Debbyanne sometimes bunked in with him overnight, after cruising the bars in Capital City, or after a late dinner date to celebrate a big score by Buck in one of his illegal, or semilegal activities. Occasionally they stayed overnight together at her place.

Little Oscar hated it when he had to share his mother with Buck at their apartment. But the big man's size was menacing, literally filling the small rooms himself. Little Oscar kept his distance and never revealed his feelings. He just bided his time, waiting and watching their relationship wax and wane, hoping it would cool off completely, and then Buck would fade out of his mother's life as so many others had done, leaving Little Oscar as her main interest again.

Buck's help with acquiring luxuries provided the difference between enjoying life, or just surviving on the welfare check that was supposed to pay the rent, provide food and clothes, plus pay the gas and electric. It never quite stretched that far with creeping inflation eroding the value of money in the seventies. Buck's help kept Debbyanne from making the rounds of the city's bars, hustling money the best way she knew how, after learning the business as one of Lonny's girls.

Debbyanne had to maintain secret hideaways to conceal all the luxury appliances Buck gave her and whatever clothes he left behind whenever he stayed

over. She never knew when the social worker would come snooping around. She didn't want deductions against her monthly check, with Buck contributing material support, cash or otherwise.

Debbyanne had met Buck in May and by August of the same year they had become a steady duo. She quickly stopped cruising the bars looking for money and companionship and saw only Buck. And since he was always horny, Debbyanne did her best to keep him satisfied, even if at times his requests bordered on kinky. She appreciated his loyalty, seeing just her and dropping his other women.

His many ways of making money occupied the rest of his time. He booked numbers, made high-interest loans, and collected for other loan sharks in addition to his own collections. Buck wasn't above dealing in dope of any kind, when the opportunity for a big score presented itself in the neighborhood. With his varied sources of income, Buck was never broke; and since he was always generous where Debbyanne was concerned, she anticipated a long and prosperous relationship. It was relaxing for Debbyanne not to worry about money, after the strain of her days with Loco, and the resulting estrangement with her former tenant neighbors. Thus Buck helped fill the social void in addition to her financial needs, as well as satisfying her in bed. Debbyanne was content for the first time since her days with Lonny.

Little Oscar was alone that warm Friday evening late in August watching a Hogan's Heroes rerun beamed into Capital City by a local nonnetwork New York City channel, laughing at the predicament of Commandant Klink, which Colonel Hogan had engineered, when he heard a key unlock the door to the

apartment. He turned to watch Buck come barging through the door with a thrusted forearm as if blocking on a running play in a football game. His odorous alcoholic wine breath filled the apartment like a sudden heat wave. After Buck glanced around the living room, with a wild-eyed, glassy haze in his eyes, rubbing himself at the fly of his pants, he asked Little Oscar, "Hey, kid, where's your mom? I need some pussy real bad." Buck's voice echoed off the walls.

"She's at the Laundromat," Little Oscar replied, letting his attention wander back to the TV show, watching Commandant Klink storm out of the prisoner barracks with Sergeant Shultz tagging behind, leaving Hogan and his cronies crowding the open doorway, smirking in obvious satisfaction at the beleaguered German officer.

"Shit—I'm too horny to wait for her." Buck rubbed the bulging object inside his pants at crotch level. "Guess you'll have to take her place, kid." His grin was slanted, his gaze leering. "Bet you got a nice soft behind, too. I think I'm gonna enjoy punking you."

Little Oscar didn't grasp Buck's meaning at first, but his approaching hulk threw an ominous shadow across the TV screen. And his wine breath got stronger. Little Oscar wrinkled his nose as he looked up in time to see Buck reach down and lift him bodily off the armchair as if the big man were picking up a feather. Little Oscar could only gape at Buck, feeling completely helpless in his hard grip. The shock stopped his breathing momentarily as Buck carried him over to the divan bed nearby and dropped him on it as if he were a small log. Little Oscar landed roughly on his stomach, making the springs squeak and the divan shake from his sudden weight on it. He wondered what was happening to him. Buck didn't look angry or mad in the face—just crazy in the eyes. But he soon realized what Buck was up to when the big man pulled down his trousers and

underwear, exposing his little boy skinny legs and bare behind.

"I'm telling my mom," was all Little Oscar could get out of his mouth, before the hard slap crashed down on him like a swinging two-by-four. It almost jerked his head off his neck, giving him an instant headache.

"Shut your fucking mouth, kid!"

Little Oscar squirmed and kicked like a young colt, but Buck stiff-armed him down. Buck's large hand acted like a steel plate pressing on his back. His chest hurt to breathe from the constant heavy pressure; and no matter how hard he tried, Little Oscar couldn't get off the divan. He flailed his arms and kicked up his feet, barely managing a half-scream before Buck slapped him harder than the first time. The blow numbed his ear and head. And the pressure on his back was still crushing him. Buck's heavy breathing sent stinking alcohol-scented breath down on him in steady waves. He tried to blow the stink away from him but failed and resorted to shallow breathing instead.

Buck used one hand to pull Little Oscar's trousers and underwear off his legs and past his toe-worn sneakers, then spread his thighs and got between them. Little Oscar's bare rear end was just below Bucks hunched, hovering torso, when he heard Buck pull down his zipper. It made a quick, snipping sound. Little Oscar glanced over his shoulder and watched Buck take out an elongated, erect penis, then spit on his fingertips and rub the saliva on the reddened tip. It looked big enough to enter a cow, instead of a small boy.

"I'm telling my mom on you," Little Oscar said again, and got slapped on the back of the head once more.

Buck bent closer and poked his wide-headed penis into the crevice of Little Oscar's crescent-shaped buttocks. It hurt each time Buck probed his anus, feeling as if a baseball bat were being shoved against him. Lit-

tle Oscar screamed with each jab. A sick ache knotted his intestines. He couldn't believe what was happening to him. Buck slapped him everytime he protested or tried to squirm out from under.

Debbyanne heard screams coming from her apartment, while climbing the stairs, then again when she was in the hallway. She barged through the open door, carrying a full plastic basket of washed and dried clothes from the Laundromat, which she dropped immediately at her feet, after grasping the reality of what she saw; Buck hunched over her half-naked son, poking at his rear end with an extended, purply-veined, blood-swollen penis.

She leaped over the basket of clothes as if she were an Olympic hurdles track star to get at Buck. She was on him in seconds, like a cat on a bird, clawing and scratching at his vested back. "You fucking degenerate!" she screeched like a mad woman. "Get away from my son!"

Buck half-turned and slapped Debbyanne across the face. She reeled sideways like a drunken woman, toppling onto the sofa against the far wall, ending up with her knees on the area rug, her torso flung over a cushion. And her head rang like the inside of a struck bell. Her eyesight blurred momentarily. She shook her head, slowly regaining her composure, before rising to her feet. When the numbness left completely, and she could think clearly again, Debbyanne ran into the kitchen where she pulled a carving knife from a utensil drawer. When she returned to the living room, Buck was still trying to sodomize her son.

"Hold still you little bugger, I can't get the head in," Buck's voice boomed across the room.

The sound of his words violated her hearing. Debbyanne held the pointed stainless steel knife at shoul-

der height, with her hands clasped around the bone handle. "If you don't get away from my son, I'm going to sink this into your heart. I mean it."

"Okay, Deb, okay. Just cool it with the blade," Buck replied, backing off the prostrate Little Oscar. "I didn't even get the head in all the way. Your kid's still cherry."

"Oh, my God, I never dreamed you'd try a sick thing like that with my son."

"Aw, come on, Deb, I'm not a sicky, just a horny."

"You're sick and you don't even know it. And to think, I really cared for you." Debbyanne lowered the knife and raised her left hand up to her temple. "Please, just get out of here and never come back. My skin crawls thinking of what you were trying to do to him." She placed the knife on the end table nearest the armchair that Little Oscar had been sitting on when Buck came barging into the apartment earlier.

Little Oscar slipped off the divan and hurriedly pulled up his underwear and trousers, then ran over to stand behind his mother. She turned to help him tuck in his polo shirt.

Then Debbyanne said to Buck, "Give me back my key. And leave. Now. I won't call the police. I'll try to forget this ever happened. But we're through, Buck. I could never let you touch me again, not after what you tried with him. And I could never trust you alone with him. It was a filthy thing to try, Buck, filthy."

"What are ya getting all bent out of shape for? He wouldn't be the first kid, or fag, I punked in the ass. I like a little variety once in *a while*. You wasn't around, so I decided the kid would have to do."

"Oh, my God, am I hearing what I'm hearing?"

Little Oscar stood behind his mother and shook like a wet dog. He couldn't stop shaking. For he could still feel the sensation of Buck's big thing poking into his

behind like a blunt-ended wooden broom handle. And the thought of it stuck up inside him had his stomach flip-flopping like clothes in a Laundromat tumbler dryer. He thought he was going to throw up right there on the rug.

Little Oscar hated Buck more at that moment than anybody else he could ever remember hating. He wished he had a gun. Because he wanted to shoot the big man down like a scroungy alley cat and get him out of their lives for good. If only his mother didn't need men and needed only him. It would be so much nicer— all the time—with her.

"Let's forget this shit, Deb. I'm thirsty. Got half a snoot full already on wine, might as well get shit-faced all the way. Go get me a beer, like a good girl. I got a few minutes to spare, before I go see a deadbeat about some money."

Debbyanne didn't move.

"Did you hear me? Read my lips, dummy. Go-get-me-a-beer."

"Maybe you didn't hear me, Buck. I said you're not welcome here anymore. And I'm not kidding. I mean it."

"I'm welcome here as long as I want to be. I've got money invested in you, bitch. Get my message, or are you hard of hearing?"

Debbyanne still didn't move.

Buck's black-lashed eyelids narrowed, his crystal-blue eyes acquiring an icy glaze. His face stiffened to a mask. "We'll see who's boss around here." He started toward Debbyanne, his thumbs hooked inside his three-inch-wide leather belt.

Little Oscar stepped in front of his mother. "I'll get-cha the beer, Buck. Don't hit my mom."

"Okay, kid, you do that for Big Buck. And you, Deb, you're sitting on the sofa with me, just like nothing

80

happened." But when Debbyanne remained where she was, Buck grabbed her broomstick-thin arm, locking his thick fingers around her bony wrist like five steel pincers. "Don't hurt me, Buck. I'm warning you," Debbyanne said, as he dragged her over to the sofa, forcing her down alongside him. Once seated, Debbyanne remained motionless and stiff, staring straight ahead at a framed print of a red barn and a field of green corn on the wall across the living room, never looking at Buck.

In the kitchen, after Little Oscar had finger-pulled open the lift tab from the top of the aluminum can, he noticed a clear plastic cylinder full of his mother's yellow-tinted sleeping capsules on the counter top in front of him. While he stared at the tubelike container, he remembered a recent TV movie and the results of what too many sleeping pills did to a character in it who had been drinking . . . like Buck. When he heard the impatient bellow of the big man demanding his beer, Little Oscar shouted back, "I got the beer, Buck, just got to open it for you."

Little Oscar pulled apart six of the capsules and poured the white powder into the can of cold beer through the small triangular opening, waiting a few more seconds to make sure the powder had a chance to dissolve, before bringing it out to Buck in the living room.

"Had a little trouble pulling off the opener, Buck. But I did it for you. See?" Little Oscar smiled widely and handed the chilled aluminum can of beer to Buck on the sofa alongside his mother.

"Now see that, Deb, your kid ain't mad at me." Buck grabbed the can of beer and immediately began gulping from the small opening in its top, making his pointed Adam's apple bob with each swallow. Some of the amber liquid dripped off his chin into his lap, wetting his black pants. He used the back of his hand to

wipe himself, and finished the first beer shortly afterwards. Debbyanne's flesh hardened, as if cut from stone. Her greenish eyes narrowed to pinpoints in her small, angular face that was framed by shoulder-length blonde hair parted in the middle at the top of her head.

"Want another beer, Buck?" Little Oscar asked.

"Yeah, kid, why not? I still got time. Still got room for more good beer." Buck glanced at the digital wristwatch on his hairy arm.

Debbyanne remained silent and stiff-backed, while digging her red-painted fingernails into the sofa cushion.

Back in the kitchen, Little Oscar dumped six more capsules into the second opened can of beer, waited for the powder to dissolve, then brought the full can out to Buck who gulped greedily at it, like a babe at its mother's breast. And again amber fluid dripped off his chin, which he hand-wiped, after coming up for air.

"You sure can drink beer, Buck," Little Oscar said.

When Buck burped, he laughed loudly and broadcasted his beer-smelling breath throughout the living room. Then he pulled at the can like a college adolescent at a beerfest. "Yeah, kid, I used to be able to drink a whole quart without stopping." When Buck finished the second can, he instructed Little Oscar, "Go get me one more, kid. Then I'm leaving. Got to keep that date with a deadbeat, who just might get his head busted, if he don't come across." Buck banged a knuckled fist into a palm and the thudding sound echoed off the walls.

Little Oscar dissolved the remaining seven capsules in the third can before bringing it out to Buck in the living room where he watched the big man swallow the brew as if he hadn't had anything liquid all day.

When Buck finished drinking the last of the beer, he belched, laughed and wiped off his chin, then slapped Debbyanne on the thigh and announced, "I'm

busting out now, but I'll be back, Deb. And you better be ready for an all-night session in the sack. I'm still feeling horny. But business before pleasure, 'cause I need the bread." He belched again, laughed and left abruptly, banging the hall door shut behind him.

Having never acknowledged his presence beside her, she didn't acknowledge his leaving, remaining rigidly stolid. But a second after he left, she catapulted herself off the sofa and ran to the door, pressing her ear against its wooden side, listening to the sound of Buck's fading footsteps down the stairs. Then she hurriedly locked the door, letting out a breathy sigh, her narrow shoulders slumping into the sleeveless print blouse she wore. "Oh, my God, why do I let myself get involved with these animals?"

When she straightened her posture, Debbyanne turned and scooped up the empty beer can off the end table next to the sofa and retreated to the kitchen with it. Little Oscar followed her like a puppy trailing its master. At the counter, Debbyanne opened the cabinet door under the sink and dropped the lightweight aluminum can into the garbage. But when she began cleaning off the counter, she discovered the empty plastic container that had held her sleeping capsules. Creases furrowed her brow. Her blonde eyebrows arched. "I just got this prescription filled yesterday." Debbyanne turned and looked at her son, who smiled up at her from under his eyebrows, the spaces showing between his front teeth. He pulled at his trouser seat.

"Honey, you didn't . . .?"

Little Oscar nodded and shifted his weight, then pulled at his seat again.

Debbyanne's frown changed to a thin-lipped smile, her brow clearing, eyes growing friendlier, opening wider to reveal more white. "Buck'll never make it across the street, after all the wine he drank before he got here, these pills, and the three beers on top of that."

"I got the idea when I saw the prescription bottle on the counter, Mom. Saw some lady do it to her husband in a movie on TV. She dumped a handful of pills into a glass of wine she gave him, and he was a goner after that. Figured it'd get rid of Buck for you. Are you glad I done it, Mom?"

". . . Yes, honey, now I am. Did that animal hurt you?"

"It was starting to, just when you came in."

"That degenerate bastard doesn't deserve to live. He'd try that again with you, when I wasn't around. Oh, God, how could I know he was that kind of a man?"

"It ain't your fault, Mom."

"It still bothers me."

"We don't need him to be happy, Mom."

"I know, honey, I know."

Little Oscar reached for his mother. They hugged there in the middle of the small kitchen next to the counter and sink for uncounted minutes, both crying soft tears. But when they heard a police car siren wailing from somewhere below them at street level, it broke their teary interlude. Separating quickly, they rushed out of the apartment and down the stairs to go see what was the matter, suspecting that Buck might be involved. From their vantage point on the high wooden porch, they could see the black and white police car, its red roof lights flashing brightly, the bigger yellow and green bus and the mixed crowd of people staring down at the street pavement near the bus stop only two blocks away.

"Go see what happened," Debbyanne whispered to Little Oscar.

He obeyed instantly, leaping off the porch steps and running down the sidewalk pavement as if a high school track star. At the accident scene, he squirmed his way through the crowd like a worm through dirt. He

got close enough to see the body lying in the street just off the curb. Little Oscar recognized the black trousers and the black leather vest and those hairy arms sticking out part way from under the bus in between the front and back wheels. He stayed long enough to watch the ambulance men drag the body out. It was Buck all right. His head was crushed and bloody, but Little Oscar could still recognize his big nose. And when they put Buck's body on the stretcher and pulled the white sheet over his face, his nose held up the bloodstained cover like a tent pole. Little Oscar left the same time the ambulance did, squirming his way out of the pressing bystanders.

"It's Buck, Mom," Little Oscar began between gasps for air, after running all the way back, "he got run over by a bus."

"You saw him?"

"Saw the men drag his dead body out from under the bus. Heard a policeman talking with a lady right next to me. She said Buck collapsed and fell in front of the bus. And then the bus driver told the cop he couldn't stop the bus in time. Buck's head got flattened like a pancake. But his big nose didn't get mashed. Was a bloody looking mess. Ugly to look at. But I couldn't stop looking, Mom." Little Oscar smiled up at his mother from under his blond eyebrows.

"That degenerate animal got what he deserved. I don't feel sorry for him. Not one bit."

"And we don't have to worry about Buck anymore now, huh, Mom?"

"Thank God no. And nobody can connect him to us, neither. And if anybody tries, I'll deny everything. They'll have to prove it, which they couldn't in a million years." Debbyanne reached for her son's hand. "Let's go upstairs, honey, I want to check you all over to make sure he didn't leave any marks on you, or hurt

you inside. You're my precious honeybunch. My only real true lover, right?"

"Love you more'n anybody else in the whole wide world, Mom."

"I know, honey, I know."

Little Oscar and his mother held hands and climbed the stairs together like smiling lovers, and with a new buoyancy in their movements.

Later, in her bedroom on the double bed, Debbyanne examined Little Oscar's naked body carefully and was satisfied that he was all right. Then she undressed and took him with her into the shower stall in the bathroom. She made sure he washed all over to rid himself of the evil touch of that degenerate, Buck. She cleansed herself of his touch also, rubbing her skin vigorously, and the parts of her body that he had used the most. She shoved the washcloth up her vagina almost as far as Buck's long penis used to get deep inside her. When she scrubbed Little Oscar's behind, he giggled at her finger probes into his anus with the washcloth, while the warm water cascaded steadily down on them like a contained waterfall.

After Debbyanne dried herself and Little Oscar, she took him back to bed with her. Little Oscar knew he was going to sleep with his mother that night. He didn't have to ask why, or whine for permission to do so. It was his reward for a job well done. And when they slid under the lightweight cotton sheet, the bedroom was still warm from the day's lingering summer heat. Debbyanne had turned on the window exhaust fan to make it bearable to sleep in the second-floor apartment bedroom.

Secure between crisp, clean sheets and safely locked in their apartment, with Buck no longer a worry, Debbyanne took her son in her arms and whispered soothing reassurance that she wouldn't let anything nasty or

filthy happen to him again, that she would always protect him and love him.

It wasn't long before she began stroking his smooth, unwrinkled skin with a light fingery touch, rotating her hand motion in a circular pattern up and down his flat stomach and abdomen. She caressed his thin, boyish arms and legs and eventually arrived at his little *pee pee,* massaging its short length until it became hard and stiffly upright like a skinny stick. Then she fondled his marble-size testicles in their fleshy sack. Soon she was kissing him on the neck and the chest and sucking at his dime-size nipples, which made Little Oscar giggle from the tickling delight it gave him. His skin tingled with each puckered kiss.

When his mother worked her way down to his navel, she circled the natural depression with her active wet tongue. It made Little Oscar's skin ripple from his toes up to his scalp, prickling it from the sensation.

Debbyanne continued downward, kissing her way an inch at a time, eventually coming to his rigid little boy's penis. And in the darkness of the bedroom, Little Oscar felt his mother's soft lips kissing it on the uncircumcised tip, then gradually down along the short shaft, while she whispered, "Mommy's kissing away all your boo-boos for you, honey."

Little Oscar giggled in pleasure, lying still like a nude statue. The covering sheet was kicked back, but he wasn't chilled by the circulating cooler night air pulled across him by the whirring window fan, which had been a present the previous month from Buck. He was warmed by his mother's naked body pressing against him. He enjoyed her loving attention, trusting her explicitly. She had returned to kissing him in a wide circle across his belly, then gradually trailed back down again to his penis and testicles. Tiny shivers undulated up his spine.

But the best part came last, when his mother's

warm mouth lowered fully on his *pee pee* and engulfed it completely in its heated wetness, which soothed him immediately.

Then his mother asked him, "Does that make you feel better, honey?"

Little Oscar giggled and replied, "I like it, Mom."

"Mommy wants you to feel better all over, honey."

Debbyanne returned her mouth on his penis and kept it there, being vertically active on it for an uncounted span of time. The sensual experience spread over Little Oscar like rings of lapping waves, working outward from his groin to his extremities.

He was inside the warm, dark, protective bubble again, contentedly alone with his mother, enjoying a happiness with her that he could never feel with any other adult. Once more blanketed by that delicate membrane with the one he cared for the most in the world—his mom—who always did *nice* things for him. He loved his mom. And being in the bubble with her was like being in heaven. No Loco, no Buck, just he and his mom. It was so nice, so beautiful, having her all to himself again. If only he could stay there forever with her—and never come out.

Chapter 3

Little Oscar watched a flight of pigeons circle his apartment building's wide square roof a number of times, before they turned abruptly and headed toward their coop roost somewhere else in the city. He liked this special feature of urban living on the four-story brick building that he and his mother were now living in since moving during September. They had lived only a year in the confining second-floor apartment in the old clapboard and brick house. He was glad his mother had decided to move again, especially after he came home with a bloody mouth from fighting three days in a row during that first week of school.

His mother couldn't afford the safer suburbs, where owning a car would be a necessity. They had to move to yet another neighborhood in Capital City. As things turned out, Little Oscar didn't really care anymore if he didn't make any new friends in this other section of the city. He now had an entire roof for a playground, with pigeons to watch and to admire. He liked the way their

heads bobbed when they walked, and the cooing sounds they made in their throats without opening their beaks.

The air was cleaner on the roof, no car and bus exhaust fumes to choke on. A breeze could always be found to cool his face, even on warmer Indian Summer days. Little Oscar liked being closer to the bright autumn sun, and to the puffy white clouds that floated above him in the navy-blue sky. It was a beautiful canopy of color that he didn't have to share with wise city kids, who didn't appreciate nice things the way he did.

Their fourth-floor rear apartment was nearest the access door to the steps that led up to the roof outlet. And right from the first day in the building, Little Oscar made the roof his very own. By the end of the first week, he had explored every inch of its flat, tarred surface; and by that November, after two months, he was as familiar with it as he was with their apartment. He'd bring up his games and toys and amuse himself for hours on Saturdays and Sundays, and most weekday afternoons after school. The roof had quickly become his friendly place away from the streets below, which had proven in the past not to be so friendly a playground for him in Capital City. All its neighborhoods were experiencing some overt form of urban decay, or had deteriorated beyond recovery with kid gangs a constant menace, as his mother was quick to claim and lament. She repeatedly said how much she missed the safety and tranquillity of the family farm, which she had to leave because of her bitchy, narrow-minded parents, and how she feared for their safety.

But Little Oscar felt safe on the roof. He knew where every vent stack was located on it, and whether the pipe was curved, straight up, capped or open. The strange sounds that came bubbling up to his ear from deep within the plumbing bowels of the multi-family apartment building fascinated him. And the assortment of TV antennas, with their weird-looking metal

piping shapes and designs, amused him. Their multitude of guy wires were attached to the two-foot-high fire wall that circled the edge of the roof, extending upward from the building's red brick exterior walls.

The wall was a source of curiosity. Its capping was worn and gritty to his touch. He liked to lean over it and study the passing parade of people and traffic some fifty feet below him. Everything and everybody looked different from up there. He liked the idea of spying on people without them knowing it, peeking into the apartment windows in the buildings next to theirs. He'd make believe he was a government secret agent, amusing himself with a spyglass made from a paper roll taken from an empty plastic wrap container.

Little Oscar was having more fun in this new setting, and was more content than ever before in his young life. He had the roof, his mother, and finally didn't have to share her with any men, since she was between boyfriends. Buck had been the last.

But with the loss of Buck's extra support, financially and socially, in bed and out of bed, Debbyanne gradually made the reluctant decision to return to *hooking* on weekends on a part-time, but steady basis. The welfare money was never enough. She had decided earlier to stay independent, and not get involved with a pimp—black, white or otherwise. She knew all the pimps who prowled the same city bars looking for new stable talent. And she had to continually reject their offers to handle her affairs in exchange for most, if not all, of her extra earnings. But in order to avoid paying for protection, and still remain independent, Debbyanne traded her services gratis to the local cops on the beat, their sergeants and lieutenants, which included doing any sex act they asked just for the privilege of working the bars in their respective beats and precincts. Her cooperation also rewarded her with ad-

vance information concerning vice squad operations. Thus she avoided jail whenever there was a politically motivated campaign by the city fathers to *bust* prostitutes in order to impress the electorate.

But a tall, lanky black pimp, nicknamed Stud, was more persistent than the other pimps she had met on her forays into the sleazy night life of Capital City. He had offered her a bigger cut of her earnings, extra protection, medical care, plus tender love and sensitive understanding, as only he knew how to give, whenever he met her out in the bars working. And when he came around to her apartment, after finding out where she lived, he brought perfume, booze and a little brown bag full of goodies, uppers and downers for whatever the mood and need. Stud knew Debbyanne had a dependency on drugs, as well as liquor, and the pressing need to make extra money, besides having men admire her and satisfy her sexually. The pills had become necessary for sleep, then to stay awake all night when working the bars. It made for a pill-taking treadmill, and it was beginning to take its toll. Debbyanne looked ten years older than her years. She couldn't get the better prices the younger hookers were asking from their tricks.

It was during that third Saturday in November of '77, a week before Thanksgiving, when Stud came by the apartment once again, just before Debbyanne left to hustle tricks at a state-sponsored real estate brokers convention being held at the biggest hotel in the city. And once again he offered his protection services, material and medical care, plus loving attention. Once again Debbyanne refused, replying, "I handle myself, Stud. If I get hassled by a cop, I just blow him on the backseat of a car, and he gets off my case. So, buzz off, please, I don't need—or want—a pimp. Besides, I don't like you, or the way you rough up your girls. I hear stories, so

eighty-six the tender loving care bullshit. Besides, why should I support your coke habit? You're even high right now, aren't you? Your eyes look wild. And I've seen you get nasty with one of your girls, when you were high on coke. So, no thanks for the offer. And if you don't mind, you know your way out, I have to shower and change clothes. Then I have to make arrangements for my son to stay with a neighbor tonight, in case I'm out late again."

"Hey, wait a minute, baby, no white-bitch-whore tells Daddy Stud to take a hike." He stiffened all of his lean, six-two physique, fingered the wide white lapels of his vested suit, then tipped his hat's wide brim up his forehead a half inch. His eyes shone like dark coals. He took two long-legged strides to where Debbyanne stood in the center of the living room and slapped her across the face with a hand as wide as a frying pan. The blow sounded like a whip slashing across a bare-skinned back. It knocked her to the rug-covered floor.

Debbyanne groaned. It was like getting hit by a flat rock. And she grunted with each succeeding blow.

"You're working for me, white bitch. You don't turn trick one, without you get my okay. You hear me—whore?"

Debbyanne couldn't reply. A punch to her ribs knocked the wind out of her, and the left side of her jaw hurt, feeling as if hit by a hammer. She sank into semiconsciousness as if groggy on drugs, rapidly falling into a mentally induced darkness. She could only lie there in pain, waiting. For what? She couldn't remember, while hoping that what she was experiencing was only a horrible dream. That it would dissipate once the pain went away.

Little Oscar stayed on the roof until it got dark after five that brisk Saturday evening in November, flip-

ping up his corduroy jacket collar against the spreading chill. He could see the early twinkling stars and the rising moon over a nearby building. He was glad it wasn't windy. But since his mother didn't want him on the roof at night, he decided to go back downstairs to the apartment.

He knew she would be going out that night to make extra money, since she didn't have a steady boyfriend to help out with their expenses, and the luxuries they'd gotten used to like everybody else. Little Oscar also knew what his mother had to do to make this extra money. He had observed her doing various sexual acts over the last few years, despite her efforts to shield him from her bedroom activities with her men.

And he resented those boyfriends and what they did to his mother. Yet he never hated her for what she did with them. It was only the men he sometimes hated enough to wish them out of his life and hers permanently, like dead, if necessary.

With the darkness settling rapidly outdoors, Little Oscar bounced happily down the stairs two at a time. The stairwell's warm air relieved his chilled face. It was even warmer in the hallway. To his surprise, he found the door to their apartment ajar. But after he stepped quickly into the living room, the scene there stopped him where he stood as if an invisible wall had dropped in front of him. Stud, the brown-skinned black pimp, dressed in his usual white suit and wide-brimmed hat, was hunched over his mother and was hitting her with hard, pounding fists as if she were a punching bag in a gym. His mother moaned with each punch that struck her head and ribs. She was a helpless lump, lying on her side, arms over her face, legs drawn up in the fetal position.

Tears leaked down Little Oscar's face in two separate streams. He ran to his bedroom closet and got his skateboard, the only weapon he could think of to use

against the towering Stud. And he whacked Stud with it on the back with all his might.

"What the fuck? Goddamn! What you doing, hitting on me, nigger boy?"

"Get away from my mother, pimp. And don't call me nigger, neither, coke junkie." Little Oscar banged Stud with the skateboard a second time.

"I'm gonna kill your skinny nigger ass!" Stud screeched, then lunged at Little Oscar, who threw the skateboard at Stud, grazing his shoulder and neck, stopping him a moment.

It was enough time for Little Oscar to make it through the front door and into the hallway. Stud chased him in long-legged pursuit, while Little Oscar pumped his short legs up the stairs to the roof outlet. A three-quarter moon bathed the entire roof in an eerie wash of light. He could see all the obstacles, besides knowing where they were from memory.

"I got you trapped now, nigger," Stud hollered in his high-pitched, reedy-sounding clarinet voice. "I'm gonna catch your skinny nigger ass and toss if off the roof like a bag of nasty shit."

Little Oscar ran in circles, ducking under guy wires, jumping over vent pipes and keeping out of Stud's long-armed reach. But when Stud did finally grab hold of his arm, Little Oscar turned quickly and kicked the tall man in the shin, then easily broke loose again.

"I'm gonna bust your nigger ass in half, you little jive turkey," Stud said, bending over and rubbing his sore shinbone.

"You gotta catch me first, pimp." Little Oscar giggled and danced away from Stud, leaping over a curved pipe vent located just five feet from the two-foot-high fire wall, before darting sideways at a ninety-degree angle like a frightened rabbit.

Stud followed his lead and leaped over the pipe also,

but his size twelve black leather boot caught the metal pipe capping by the toe. He did an awkward somersault in a headlong spin through the chilled night air. His arms went straight out to keep his head from hitting the roof. And the white hat he wore sailed off his head, landing brim up on the tarred surface against the brick fire wall. Stud's protective action only worked to make him do a handstand, then flipped him completely over. He landed hard on his rear end on top of the wall, with his long legs dangling over it. Inertia tumbled him the rest of the way forward. He managed to turn his body enough to grasp the gritty, abrasive capping block with one hand, then the other. His hold was tenuous, gradually slipping to his fingertips, dangling fifty feet above the concrete-paved alley.

"Help me, kid. Grab my arms. Hurry, man, I'm slipping!" Stud's voice squeaked at every word.

Little Oscar could see the whites of Stud's eyes. "Fuck you, pimp," he replied, then slammed his fists down as hard as he could against Stud's fingertips.

Stud screamed all the way down. He hit the concrete with a thud. Then there was immediate silence. But the sound void was soon filled with city noises, street traffic from beyond the alley and a jet plane's roar from the dark sky above.

Little Oscar peered down into the poorly lit alleyway. There was one small light over the side entrance to the other building. Stud's white-suited form lay spread-eagled on the killing surface. Little Oscar stared at him a long time. Stud never moved, never cried out in pain.

Figuring he was one dead pimp, Little Oscar mumbled to himself, "I'm glad. Won't never hit on my mom again."

Little Oscar stood away from the wall. His blood-warmed face cooled in the night breeze. It would be a pleasure to report the pimp's death to his mother. Be-

fore he left, he deliberately stepped on Stud's wide-brimmed white hat, giggling as he did it, then circled the nearby vent pipe that Stud had tripped over and walked slowly back to the exit door. He stepped carefully down the steep stairs to the fourth-floor hallway. The air inside the building warmed his skin. Sweat trickled down his sides from under his arms.

His mother was still lying on the living room rug. He got her to sit up, wincing when he saw her bruised face. A mousey-looking lump had formed already under her left eye on her once-pretty face.

"Mom, Stud's dead. He won't be back to beat up on you no more. He fell off the roof. Looks like a dead white bird down there in the alley. Ain't we lucky? That pimp is one dead man for sure now. Flew over the wall and landed smack on the concrete like a sack of potatoes. He ain't moving at all now. Got to be dead. I'm gonna have to call the police. But it was an accident, Mom. I didn't do nothing . . . this time . . . to make it happen. He tripped over a pipe. I just got lucky. I mean we got lucky. He tried to hang on the wall, and asked me to help hold him, but I wouldn't. Not after what he did to you. But I'm not telling the police that."

"Don't call the police, honey. I'm afraid of them." His mother's voice was low and hurt-sounding, like a little girl's, who's been spanked for being naughty.

"We have to, Mom. But we got nothing to be afraid of . . . this time. We're in the clear. It was an accident. Mostly. And he was a no-good pimp anyway. The cops'll be glad he got killed. One less pimp around to beat up on women."

"I know, honey. You saved my life."

"You're my mom, I'd do anything for you."

"Thank you."

"I love you, Mom."

"I know, honey, I know. And I love you."

They hugged for a long time, with Debbyanne sitting up on the rug, and Little Oscar beside her on his knees.

Little Oscar took charge and got his mother off the rug and onto the nearby sofa to wait for the police, whom he called to report the accident.

While they waited for the police to arrive, Little Oscar wrapped ice cubes in a plastic bag and a towel and gently placed the ice pack on his mother's left cheek. The swelling had gotten worse. She looked like the losing prizefighter after a boxing match. When she said she couldn't stand the cold ice pack any longer, Little Oscar applied a damp cool cloth to her bruised face, then dried it with a towel. He even combed her hair. Afterward, insisting she put the ice pack on her face again, he held it for her whenever her arm got tired.

And that was how the police found them when they arrived at the apartment, Little Oscar still attending to his battered mother.

He willingly escorted the policemen up to the roof and showed them just how the accident happened, explaining the reasons why along the way. When Little Oscar looked over the wall again, he watched the ambulance personnel take Stud away on a stretcher, while the red roof lights flashed a crimson brightness into the semidark alleyway.

Later, when they returned to the apartment, the policemen asked more questions of Little Oscar and his mother. But after examining Debbyanne, they were easily satisfied with the answers, that it really was an accident, leaving soon afterwards. It was a double relief to Little Oscar, watching the police leave and knowing that the nasty-ass, coke-using pimp wouldn't be back to bother his mother ever again. Now he could take care of her in peace, get her cleaned up and feeling

good again. It made him happy inside just to know he could help her. That she could depend on him.

He convinced his mother she should take a warm bath, since she wouldn't be going out, not in her hurt condition. It would soothe her sore arm muscles and ease the hurt in her back and ribs, where Stud had punched her. Then she could go to bed and rest and recover faster from the beating. After she readily agreed, Little Oscar led her into the bathroom. He helped her undress and filled the tub with hot water, pouring in bath salts and oily skin lotion for added luxury. Little Oscar helped his mother wash her back and talked to her the whole time she was immersed in the heated water and soaking the soreness out of her muscles. When she got out of the tub, he helped her towel off, then led her into the bedroom and pulled back the bedcovers for her.

"Don't leave me alone tonight, honey. Sleep with me," Debbyanne said to Little Oscar, her voice small and high, like a little girl's.

Little Oscar didn't have to be asked twice, quickly undressing and crawling under the blanket and sheet to be with his mother, his naked little boy's body pressing close against her adult female nakedness. She smelled of perfumy bath salts and skin lotion and fragrant body cologne that she had splashed on herself in the bathroom. He loved to smell it on her. They hugged as soon as he got into bed with her, like long-lost lovers finding each other once again.

Little Oscar loved it when his mother let him sleep with her. Only this time he took charge, caressing her clean, smooth skin with long, gentle, sliding hand and arm motions, like a horizontal pendulum. He whispered soothing words of reassurance in her ear, with her silky soft hair brushing against his lips; that he would always protect her and no pimp or anybody else

Little Oscar obeyed his mother, climbing on top of her, then slipping in between her legs, and meshing his nakedness with hers, while his mother's hand guided his short, rigid, little boy's penis into her. And after penetration to its fullest, her warm, moist flesh became a living sponge around his heated, dry, blood-filled organ. He followed her lead. They butted against each other in a slow, rhythmic pelvic motion as if they were adult lovers. It wasn't long before his mother moaned as if hurt, writhing in spasmlike, muscle-tightening movements under him. Her arms wrapped tightly around his narrow back, her sharp fingernails digging into his flesh like nails as she gasped her breathy excitement into his ear, her warm breath tickling him.

"Oh, honey, you did it so good for mommy."

His mother's arms went limp and fell to the bed. But Little Oscar continued to hug his mother. He never wanted to let go. With his ear to her chest, he could hear her rapid heartbeat, and feel her body heat against his cheek.

Little Oscar was proud and happy at having satisfied his mother as so many other men had done in the past. He was just as good for her as they had been.

Although he relaxed his hold on his mother, he remained on top of her, feeling once again the bubble envelop him, enjoying her warm and intimate closeness. He was experiencing the kind of contentment and satisfaction that only his mother could muster up for him. He gladly let the bubble engulf him once more like a cocoon of soft air surrounded by a thin, transparent membrane of water. It was always a happy place for him in its embrace. And now with his mom as close as was physically possible, he savored every second of time in the bubble, knowing it wouldn't, couldn't last forever. That when the next man eventually intruded into his mother's life, and his, it would burst the bubble for him once more.

He hated that the most. Hated those big strangers taking his mother's attention away from him. Hated their bigness, and their big penises, too, that gave his mother so much pleasure.

"My honeybunch, my lover," his mother whispered in his ear.

"I love you, Mom," Little Oscar whispered back.

They hugged again, not as hard, but firmly. And Little Oscar wished he could crawl back up inside his mother all the way—and never come out.

Chapter 4

It was almost a rerun of her last odyssey home to the farm for Debbyanne, eleven years ago to the day from that distant Friday, December 16, 1966 when she was pregnant with Little Oscar. Only now she was accompanied by her son on his birthday this Friday, December 16, 1977. And their last hitchhiking ride had also been in a pickup truck with Debbyanne making the driver let them out on Creek Road at the same place she'd gotten out that other time, a thousand feet from the Pleasanton-Mt. Lebanon Road intersection. Then she and Little Oscar walked in the raw, late autumn weather that was threatening to bombard them with rain or snow. The sky had thickened considerably since they left Capital City. A dark layer of gray clouds hung overhead like a blanket of dirty cotton, similar to the last time she had returned home swollen with Little Oscar inside her.

"Why'd we get out here, Mom?" Little Oscar asked

his mother, seeing nothing but woods and fields around them.

"I wanted to show you the exact way I came back to the farm, that day I had you in the tractor shed."

Little Oscar nodded, following his mother through the waist-high brush and the taller naked-limbed trees that flanked the road and the split-rail fencing surrounding her parents' farm. Dry brown leaves and fallen branches crackled under their boots with each slow step.

"Look, honey, here's the spot where I took the top and middle rails off the fence and climbed over the lower one. And was I big in the belly with you. It was hard on me walking over this rough ground."

"They never put the fence rails back up, Mom?"

"I wonder why? They're still on the ground where I left them."

"And looking all rotted. The rest of the fence needs fixing, too."

"It does. And the field looks like it didn't get planted this past summer," Debbyanne replied. After a pause, she added, "Come on, honey, let's go up to the tractor shed."

Little Oscar followed his mother over the uneven ground that was covered with dead weeds and dormant rye grass. Minutes later they came to a wooden building that was ready to fall down with one good shove or strong gust of wind.

"Oh, my God, the roof's fallen in! We can't even go inside it." Debbyanne's voice was shrill.

"Is this the tractor shed, Mom?"

"Was is more like it. You were born in there eleven years ago today. And the weather was just as raw and threatening back then."

Little Oscar squinted in the glary gray daylight, flipping up the collar on his corduroy jacket, then picked at the seat of his jeans. The wind had grown

gusty during the few minutes they had stood near the tractor shed.

Debbyanne turned and surveyed the nearby farm outbuildings. The dull-looking, weathered red barn had some of its wide vertical side boards missing. The corncrib was empty. The chicken coop was silent and slanted at a ten degree list. The garage had boards rotted at ground level. And the packing shed looked unused recently also. Even the farmhouse appeared neglected. All the buildings needed a painting. Bare wood showed through wherever the previous coat of paint had flaked, peeled, or blistered.

"I don't like the looks of things. My father must not be keeping up with repairs like he used to. The farm was always spotless, and the buildings kept up. It looks more like Li'l Abner's Dogpatch now. Really got run down. A lot more than when I came back the last time," Debbyanne said, her voice trailing away as if she were speaking more to herself than to her son.

"It sure don't look like a pretty farm, Mom."

"At least the hills and the woods still look the same. Over there's the creek, inside that strip of trees and brush. I used to play Robinson Crusoe there, and fish for trout and bass. Or just hide from my father, when I did something he didn't like, which was most of the time, and he was after me to whack hell out of my behind."

"We going up to the house now, Mom?"

"Yes, and won't my folks be surprised to see us."

They approached the rear shed door to the farmhouse in silence; and when Debbyanne knocked hard on its wooden plank surface, it shook on its metal hinges. Finally, after four more poundings, the door was unlocked and flung open.

Debbyanne stared in shocked silence at the aged apparition of her father. He had less wispy white hair on

his pink, scaly scalp and more creases and deeper folds hanging on his jowly face. His bleary blue eyes looked rheumy, their remembered sparkle missing. His faded denim overalls were patched at the knees. The red checked flannel shirt he wore was ripped at the collar. And his work boots sported dried mud on them. He was stooped and looked a lot shorter than Debbyanne remembered him to be.

"So, it's you," her father said, "and what brings you back after all these years? You must want something. That's the only time children come around to see their parents nowadays, after they bleed them dry."

His voice sounded whispery, with a raspy edge to it. Debbyanne decided that the wind must've gone out of his ornery sails sometime ago.

"I came back to see you and mom. You're still my parents. We're still family. And I brought my son, Oscar, with me to meet his grandparents, now that he's old enough to remember."

Little Oscar took his cue from his mother and stepped in front of her. He smiled up to the old man who was his grandfather. His mother placed a hand on each of his shoulders.

"Honey, this is your grandfather."

"Hi," Little Oscar said, smiling widely, revealing his spaced front teeth.

The old man frowned deeper lines across his reddened brow and grunted. Then he said to Debbyanne, "Looks like his father must've looked. And you wouldn't listen to me—would you?"

Debbyanne didn't answer her father and Little Oscar stopped smiling.

Then a round-shouldered, white-haired woman came into the shed and stood next to the old farmer. She had on a washed-out, colorless apron over a faded housedress that made it difficult to tell the print pattern from background color of the garment.

"Hi, Mom, meet your grandson, Oscar. He was only an infant the last time you saw him."

"We can see him. Just 'cause we wear bifocals don't mean we're blind," her father replied in a raspy voice, turning to stare at his wife. The white-haired woman nodded agreement, but remained silent, while staring at Little Oscar with eyes that looked owlish and exaggerated behind the thick-lensed eyeglasses.

"Aren't you going to invite us in? We've come a long way to see you. And we're tired and hungry." Debbyanne looked at her mother, then at her father.

"We don't care how far you came, or how hungry you are," he replied. "You left here ten years ago of your own free will. So you can stay away permanently, far as we're concerned. Both you and your nigger bastard can go to hell!"

Debbyanne's father slammed the shed door in their faces. Little Oscar jumped under his mother's hands. They could hear the couple retreating toward the kitchen, after locking the shed door behind them, then closing and locking the kitchen door also.

Debbyanne couldn't believe what was happening for a moment, before she screamed, "You haven't changed. You're still a son-of-a-bitch! I won't forget this. I hope you croak, you prejudiced old bastard!" She pounded on the closed shed door with her fists, shaking the shed wall.

Little Oscar stood next to his mother and could feel her trembling thin body against him. He hurt inside for her. His stomach acids bubbled like boiling soup, while his intestines twisted and ached for food, with breakfast the last remembered meal that day, eaten some eight hours ago. He wiped away eye-blurring tears with his hands, wishing he had a knife, or a gun, thinking that he'd stab or shoot those two old folks to death; and without a second thought for what they did to his mother just then, treating her as if she were a disease.

He knew he would never forget it. The scene was burned into his memory as if done with a red-hot branding iron. And he'd especially remember the way that ugly old ruddy-faced man glared down at him as if he were a cockroach. Little Oscar could taste the anger in his dry mouth, feel the hate burn his eyes. But he had deep sorrow and pity inside him for his helpless mother, who was getting more helpless lately in her dealings with adults. She was safe now only with him. And he promised himself that he would protect his mother from these big people who were always hurting her with their fists, or with their nasty-mouthed tongues.

When it became obvious that her parents weren't going to let them into the farmhouse, Little Oscar said, "They don't want us here, Mom. Let's go on back where we belong, before it gets colder."

"You're right, honey. The weather looks like it's going to dump something on us, if we don't get out of it soon."

"Yeah, and we got a lot of walking and hitchhiking ahead of us, before we get home."

"I know, honey. And I'm really sorry things didn't work out for us, like I'd planned—and hoped."

Little Oscar nodded understanding and led his mother around the farmhouse toward the front of the property. He sensed busy eyes were watching them from the nearby shade-drawn windows, but said nothing to his mother. The hurt was already sharp enough for her to bear.

"I thought they'd let us stay with them for at least a week or two," Debbyanne said to Little Oscar. "I needed a break away from our life in the city. My nerves are tight. I feel like I'm about to come unglued. And Christmas would've been so nice and relaxing for me in the country. For you, too, honey. And you wouldn't have missed that much school. We could've gone for long

healthy walks in the fresh air. And if it snowed, nothing prettier than a white Christmas on the farm. But they've always ruined my plans. Even when I was a little girl. Specially him. I should've known better. But I was desperate, after what Stud did to me. Oh, God, I hope that bastard's burning in hell!"

"No use thinking about Stud, Mom, and what happened in the past. We just better hurry and get back home to the city, where we belong. I'm cold and hungry, and my feet are tired."

"We'll get a ride once we get to the highway. Truck drivers always stop for women."

"We got a long walk ahead of us first."

"Maybe we'll get lucky and get a ride on Creek Road."

"I sure hope so, Mom."

But they didn't get a ride on Creek Road. It was an exhausting hike in the cold weather over that five-mile stretch of country road to the four-lane concrete highway. And by the time they made it there, sore-footed, hungry, with throats parched, the weather had turned from just threatening to rain, harder than they expected. It changed to sleet by their first ride south from a van driver, penetrating their upturned jacket and coat collars. The frosty cold pellets of iced water sent freezing sensations down their necks. A chilling wetness soon saturated their hair and scalps. They were miserable climbing into the van for the first of many rides, the longest in tractor trailers, with their leering drivers, before they made it to Capital City after midnight, sneezing their way up the stairs to their fourth-floor apartment like stumbling drunks. During the arduous climb, Little Oscar suggested aspirin, hot tea with honey and hot baths, then quickly to bed. Debbyanne readily agreed.

Once in their apartment, where the heat was immediately comforting, they still couldn't stop shaking. They left a trail of wet clothing across the living room, the bedroom and into the bathroom, where Little Oscar helped his mother fill the tub with hot water. They soaked in it together, letting the heated water seep into their tight muscles and chilled bones, until their skins wrinkled and they resembled a couple of oversized prunes.

After toweling off, it was flannel pajamas, terry cloth bathrobes, tube socks and soft, fluffy slippers.

But Little Oscar had to stop his mother from taking sleeping capsules along with the brandy she had poured copiously into her tea with honey, reminding her what had happened to Buck under the bus. He got her to settle for just brandy, tea with honey and a couple of aspirin, before they crawled into bed, snuggling close to each other under the blankets, but still shivering, still thawing out from the cold that had penetrated deep inside them.

"I'm so cold, honey, I'm never going to get warm again," Debbyanne whispered in a shaky voice.

"We'll get warm again, Mom, if we got to stay in bed all day tomorrow."

"I should've realized my father wouldn't change. That he still wouldn't want us around. And would never forgive me for not giving you up to the state for adoption. My running away again only added salt to the wound. I always defied him. And he never forgives. Boy—does he hold a grudge!"

"You couldn't know he'd still be mean and nasty to you, Mom. But we still got each other, for always and always. And we don't need anybody else, neither. Because nobody cares about us anyway, like we do about each other. Right, Mom?"

"You're right, honey. And thank you for taking such good care of me."

"I love you, Mom."

"You are truly my honeybunch."

Debbyanne hugged Little Oscar closer to her and they remained that way under the bed covers for a long time, shivering like two stray dogs in a snow-covered alley, before they finally fell asleep in each other's arms.

Lying there in his mother's embrace before he dozed off, feeling her softness close to him and enjoying the scent of her cologne and body powder, he wished he could build a fire inside them to get warm and dry forever, and to get his mother feeling good and healthy again.

Because he was worried about other matters concerning his mother besides their present misery.

She was drinking too much lately, and always taking drugs to get through her days and nights. She wasn't eating right and never enough, either, always leaving food on her plate when she did cook for them, even if it was only a TV dinner.

And her face didn't look right to him. It was too thin and sunken-in at her cheekbones. Her skin looked pale and sickly. She used layers of makeup to put color back into her cheeks.

His mother was always sick with colds lately. He wanted her healthy and happy and beautiful again. Their getting soaked to the skin worried him. It would give his mother a worse cold now. He just knew it would. He lay there next to his mother with his eyes closed and hoped and prayed, mumbling the prayers under his breath that his mother had taught him, that he could get her through the bad times. It was all that he could do at the moment, silently hope and hurt and love his mother, and be the man she needed so badly.

He was determined to be the one and only man in her life, keeping it that way for ever and ever. He loved his mother that much, and never wanted to leave her,

even after he grew up. Little Oscar was content to be with her in the city, or anywhere else. He didn't care that her parents wouldn't let them stay on the farm. It was only the principle of the rejection that hurt. He'd never forget it. And he'd never forgive those old people for hurting his mother's feelings—and his, too.

Chapter 5

Little Oscar and Debbyanne spent a quiet Christmas Sunday in their apartment, and happily for him it was without any intruding boyfriends hanging around to steal his mother's attention away. It was pure delight to have his mother all to himself on such an important day.

They played his new games that he'd gotten for Christmas presents, purchased with some of the welfare check money, since Debbyanne hadn't earned any extra money *hooking* in over a month, ever since Stud's brutal beating. And Little Oscar could now look at his mother's face without wincing at the purplish bruise marks and distorted swelling around her eyes and nose, which had finally cleared.

They played the shorter version of Monopoly first. Little Oscar won, getting all of his mother's property and money. Then they played Clue. Again Little Oscar won, guessing the murderer, the weapon and the place

everytime before his mother could. But she won the game, Masterpiece, acquiring more of the expensive paintings than he did, and didn't get stuck with any of the forgeries. Little Oscar was glad his mother won the game. It made her laugh and smile again, more so than she had done since Stud and their ordeal returning from her parents' farm that miserabie Friday night over a week ago.

Debbyanne's immediate reaction to that final rejection by her parents was to numb herself with alcohol. And her persistent cough and lingering cold enforced the rationale to fight the weakness with brandy, whiskey or vodka dumped generously into her coffee, tea or straight without any chaser. The cheapest brands were all she could afford, since she had to buy for herself. She needed money also for her sleeping pill habit at night, and for her tranquilizer habit by day. Food had last priority, especially during her depressed moods. At mealtimes, Little Oscar always finished eating first, even after consuming all the leftovers, while Debbyanne only picked at the hamburger stew on her plate, or whatever else their simple fare consisted of for the evening meal. Cheapest to buy and easiest to prepare were the standards she sought as a homemaker fulfilling her obligations to cook for them.

All she could afford for their Christmas dinner, after spending more than she should have for the games and some needed shirts and pants for Little Oscar, while splurging and buying a new hair dryer for herself, was hot dogs, baked beans out of a can and deli-prepared potato salad and cole slaw. Debbyanne ate half a hot dog, a forkful of beans, some cole slaw and very little of the potato salad, while Little Oscar had seconds of everything.

And to Little Oscar's continued delight, it was a private affair, since they didn't get, or expect, any company. Debbyanne's waning sociability made for

minimum contact with the other tenants, while Little Oscar kept to himself, playing mostly on the roof, or watching TV in the apartment. When he left the building, it was to go to school or to shop for his mother at a neighborhood corner grocery store where the prices were always higher than at the nearest supermarket in another distant section of the city. So her welfare money never lasted the entire month. They always ended up buying food on credit during the last week of every month.

Little Oscar did all the grocery shopping for his mother. The only buying she did was for whiskey, brandy, or vodka at the neighborhood package goods store where she also had a running credit tab account. Little Oscar even bought the small artificial plastic Christmas tree and decorated it with golf ball-size red, blue and yellow plastic Christmas balls plus the usual silver tinsel, placing it on an end table in a corner of the living room, then grouping the presents around it on Christmas Eve. Anything to cheer up the place for his mother, that sad holiday season. He was taking charge oftener and making more family decisions, gradually becoming the man of the house at age eleven and acting more like fifteen where it concerned his mother's welfare and his own.

But he still couldn't get his mother to cut down on her drinking and drug habits. At every excuse she indulged in either one. And since her cold never cleared up, settling deeper into her chest, with a throat-wracking, persistent cough, making her voice constantly hoarse, she was either drinking continually to fight the cold by day, or popping pills to sleep at night. She never mixed the two, heeding Little Oscar's warnings and remembering Buck's fatal encounter with the combination.

Along with her alcoholic glow, Debbyanne became more loquacious than ever, venting her feelings about

her parents in a daily litany of hate, with Little Oscar as her audience of one. It usually began during lunch with a repeat at suppertime, if Little Oscar couldn't get her mind off her parents and to playing with the new games she'd gotten him for Christmas.

"My wonderful parents got tired of the steady grind of running a farm and raising a bunch of kids by the time I came along. I was a change-of-life baby. My mother had me in her late forties. So I must've been a real surprise to everybody. I think they not only resented having me, but actually hated me for keeping them tied down and having to be parents a lot longer, raising one more brat late in their lives. My brothers and sisters were going to high school and college, when I came along. I was the final burden in a long line of burdens. Farm life is nice only when you don't have to work at raising crops and animals to scratch out a living and send kids to college, besides. It can grind you into the ground like an earthworm. You age before your time, working your butt off year in and year out, with no letup. Not even in winter. There's always something to be done."

When Debbyanne paused in her monologue, she took another hit from the glass of rye whiskey and water chilled with ice cubes, then continued her family history spiel at the kitchen table, with Little Oscar, his chin resting on his palms, elbows propped on the table, as her captive audience.

"Never had a dress, a coat, or even a pair of goddamn panties that I could say my parents bought for me. I wore nothing but hand-me-downs from my older sisters. I even came back to the farm to have you wearing some lady's discards. That's why today I won't wear anybody's clothes. I buy my own. I hated wearing somebody else's all the time. I wanted my own things. But let's not forget put-downs. I suffered my share up there.

And that was because I never did anything right for them, whether I was helping my grouchy father feed or milk the cows, slop the pigs, clean out the manure in the barn, whatever. And if I just stood outside the chicken coop, my eyes burned from the wicked ammonia smell in the chicken droppings. When I went inside to clean up, I'd throw up the whole time I was in there. Then while I was resting, I had to help my mother clean the house, weed the garden and wash and iron clothes till my goddamn arms fell off. I'd get so weak after awhile, I couldn't lift the iron. Only then would she let me rest, the witch. I was the unpaid domestic help and farmhand. And strictly unappreciated. Like I had to do it. The others were smart. They got off the farm as soon as they could, getting active in high school activities that kept them away from the chores. Later on they all went to one college or another and stayed away permanently after graduating, getting jobs in cities in other states. They're scattered now all over the country. The closest one's in Chicago. They were always like strangers to me. Four brothers and sisters and I don't really know any of them. They never cared about me. I was just the little nuisance to escape from, or put up with. I've got blood relatives who don't give a good goddamn whether I live or die. Only you, honey, only you care about me."

"That's right, Mom," Little Oscar replied. "That's why we've got to love each other, and take care of each other. It's important, 'cause we only got us—now."

"Yes, honey, we do love each other. At least I know that for sure. But I don't think any man's ever really loved me just for me. Maybe your father cared for me in his own special way. But the others just used me and my body. Yet, I don't really care, because I used them back. It was a fair exchange. But my parents are a different story. They always grabbed from me, never gave back. Took my love, my labor, my time, my affection,

117

my caring and my feelings. You name it, they yanked it from me with both hands like it was their goddamn right as my wonderful parents, the ingrates. But did they ever once make me feel loved or wanted, or even appreciated? No, never. And I mean never. Not one goddamn time! It eats my insides out everytime I think about it."

Debbyanne paused to drink eagerly from her glass of whiskey and water, closing her eyes and never stopping for breath.

Little Oscar observed his mother and decided he didn't like what he saw; ashen complexion with sunken cheeks and dark circles under her eyes. And her coughing was getting worse. The weakness was showing on her drawn face. She had lost more weight than she could afford. She was the thinnest he could remember, almost skin and bones, no shape anymore to her hips, just a living, walking, breathing broomstick.

"The only time I ever enjoyed myself on the farm," Debbyanne continued, "was when I did something I wanted to do." Her hoarse voice sounded angry and deep and low in tone, contrasting with the small frail body it came out of as she pounded a fist on the table. "Like when I raised a baby goat my father wanted to let die, after it was born and the mother died giving birth to it. And when it was full grown, the son-of-a-bitch sold it. Not caring one bit that it was my pet. Then I raised a newborn calf that was rejected by its mother. And didn't my father sell it for veal, and never once said thanks to me for helping save the calf. I fed it milk out of a bottle, holding it in my arms and talking softly to it like it was a baby. It was so cute and big-eyed. I felt bad when my father sold it to the slaughterhouse—the poor thing—to be killed and eaten by people. Makes my skin crawl when I think about it. My father never paid me a cent anytime I helped him out like that. That's why I had to run down to the woods

and get away from the farm work once in a while, to have some fun and a quiet moment to myself. It was so peaceful in the woods, with only the sounds of nature. Birds chirping. Insects buzzing. The creek water splashing over the rocks. I used to make a lean-to out of branches and leaves, then make a campfire and cook bacon fat over it and let the drippings fall onto a piece of bread. Um, it was good. And I used to catch rainbow trout and smallmouth bass. The creek always had fish in it. The state fish and game man used to stock it every couple months. And whatever I caught, I'd cook it over the fire, like an Indian. Oh, I was the happiest in the woods."

Debbyanne finished the last of her drink, then made herself another: heavy on the whiskey, light on the water.

Little Oscar frowned, wishing his mother would drink less. It seemed anymore she was never without a glass in her hand.

"When I grew up, I couldn't date. Couldn't go dancing, or have a date visit me at the house. My parents said it was sinful to have my body rub against a boy's. They really gave me the benefit of the doubt, didn't they? My wonderful parents got religion late in life, so I had to put up with their craziness. A couple of times I snuck out and hitched a ride on Saturday night to the school dances. And it was after the last beating I'd gotten from my father, that I decided to bust out at age sixteen and hitched a ride down here to Capital City. Not long after that I met your father and got pregnant with you, honey."

"You liked living with my father?"

"Yes, honey, he was the only man I can say I really came close to being in love with. Only thing we didn't live that long together, before he got killed in a street fight, protecting me. It happened on a hot, humid summer night outside a rough neighborhood bar where a

lot of punks hung out. We were walking by minding our own business, when they started needling us, his being black and my being white. Then one thing led to another and a fight started, after one of those animals grabbed me by the arm. It was terrible. They jumped Oscar and stabbed him, then ran, leaving him on the sidewalk bleeding his life away for me. i was so upset, I couldn't remember anything about their faces, or their clothes, or anything else, when I got questioned by the cops. They never caught any of those punks. Those murderers. They must've left town till the heat wore off. A lot of punks get away with murder in this city. And it's getting more and more dangerous to live around here. Too many junkies keeping their habits going at fifty dollars a day. They'll rob their own mothers to get money to buy dope."

Little Oscar nodded agreement with his drunken mother. At least he had the roof for his safe playground high above the city's dangerous streets. Nobody bothered him up there.

Then Debbyanne placed her hands over her eyes and shaking her head, exclaimed, "Oh, God, I hate my parents! And nobody would believe my hate for them." She removed her hands and looked at her son. "Only you, honey, only you. Slamming that door in our faces and telling us to go to hell. If I had a gun in my hand, I'd have shot the old bastard ten times in the head just to make sure he died on the spot."

"And I would've helped you hold the gun, Mom."

"I know, honey. But it just galls me, their locking the shed door, and then the kitchen door, to make sure we couldn't get in their fucking house. And then staying inside like we were common burglars skulking around their precious property. I'm surprised they didn't call the police. They treated us like we had the black plague. Their own flesh and blood. I know they

never forgave me for having you, and for running away again, and for everything else I did. Their hate for me really lingered. Maybe they still haven't forgiven themselves for having me."

"Can parents hate their children, Mom?"

"You better believe it, honey. Oh, I wish I had the strength, I'd go back up there and burn their farm down to the ground. Get the whole goddamn place going up in flames like one big bonfire. I'd do it late at night, when my parents would be sleeping upstairs. The clapboards on the old house are dry from age. They'd light up like matchsticks. The house would be blazing in minutes. My parents wouldn't have a chance to escape. The old bastards would be caught upstairs. They'd burn to death in seconds. God, I can see the orange and red flames now and feel the heat on my face and hear their screams for help. It'd be the only way I could make them suffer. Make them pay for rejecting me—and you, honey. It's the only way I could destroy their ratty farm and barbecue them like a couple of hot dogs. I wish I had the strength, I'd really go up there and torch the whole goddamn place. I really would."

"What about getting caught by the police, Mom?"

"So what if I got caught? They'd only put me in jail. My life's been one big jail. Besides, they'd have to prove it. And who'd be a witness? The dead cows and chickens? But it'd be worth going to jail over. Getting revenge on my rotten, selfish parents. Oh, how I'd love to do it."

"It would be something to see, Mom."

"Would you help mommy do it, honey?"

"Sure would, Mom. I'd help you burn down their stupid farm."

"Thank you, honey. I know you'd stick by your mommy. But it's only talk. I just don't have the strength to do it now. But God's going to punish them

for me later when they die and go straight to hell, and burn for their sins against me—and you, honey, for ever and ever in eternity."

Whenever Debbyanne made a hate tirade against her parents, it always left her weak, consuming most of her strength. Then she'd lapse into periods of silence, which she did that afternoon during that last week of December. But after this last particularly lengthy speech, she fell into a noisy coughing spell and needed half of a bottle of whiskey to get the tickle out of her throat. And when she complained of being too weak to stand, Little Oscar helped her into bed. Once there, she complained of chest pains. All Little Oscar could do was to cover her with blankets and worry in silence. Her breathing grew progressively difficult and labored.

In a short while, Debbyanne complained of being hot and tossed the blankets off herself. She soon vacillated from chills and chattering teeth, which Little Oscar thought sounded like a baby's rattle, to overheated sweating, with blotchy red spots forming on her cheeks and forehead. Little Oscar took his mother's temperature that afternoon. It registered 105 degrees Fahrenheit during one of her hot spells, which frightened him. He hurriedly placed cloth compresses soaked in cold water on her forehead. At her suggestion, he rubbed her arms, neck, chest, back and legs with rubbing alcohol. He hated the smell of it. But only minutes later, she complained of chills again, and he hurried to cover her with blankets to keep off drafts. The apartment was never warm enough when Debbyanne had chills.

Little Oscar spent most of his Christmas recess nursing his mother. And when she failed to improve, he decided not to go back to school the following week, hoping to nurse his mother back to health himself.

He did everything to make sure she remained in bed and rested. He cooked canned chicken broth with

egg noodles and vegetable soup for her and helped her eat it when she complained she was too weak to lift the spoon to her mouth, usually after coughing spells that left her limp and pale.

During quieter moments, he just held her hand and talked softly to her, or listened to her stories, although sometimes she didn't make any sense in what she said.

He couldn't help notice when he held her hand that the fingernails were bluish. Even her lips looked blue. Minus makeup, her face was a shocking, bloodless white with contrasting sunken eyes and dark circles under them, the chicken skin sagging and puffy. He wanted to cry at the sight of her. But he just bit his lower lip instead and sucked it in when he drew blood.

Later, when he suggested getting a doctor to see her, or that maybe he should call for an ambulance to take her to the hospital, Debbyanne got upset and ordered him not to call anybody, declaring she wasn't that sick. That it was just a bad cold. That she'd get better with bed rest, her whiskey and her little honeybunch, who was taking such good care of her, while admitting she had a fear of hospitals, doctors and nurses. That she'd never come home alive again, once she got into their clutches.

The next day, a Wednesday, during that first week of January, 1978, Little Oscar sensed his mother was more than just suffering from a bad cold, when she started spitting up a rusty-colored phlegm. It made him sick to clean out the plastic bucket he used to catch the slimy stuff that came gurgling out of her lip-fluttering mouth. And each spitting spell left her weaker than the last. She labored for breath as if doing a day's hard physical labor, her thin chest heaving for air. She passed if off to him as just a sign that all the congestion inside her was finally coming out. That now for sure she would get better without having any blood-sucking doctors and sarcastic nurses fooling around with her.

By nightfall, Debbyanne complained, "My chest hurts again, honey. I can't stand the pain this time. Help me get better, please help me, honey."

Little Oscar nodded and assured her he would. But in reality all he could do was sit helplessly at her bedside and pat her hand that was cold and limp to his touch. And the nails looked bluer than the previous day.

That was during one of her more lucid moments.

Soon afterwards she babbled about the creek water being too cold on her feet and legs, and how much trouble she was having freeing her fishing line that was stuck around a rock. Later, she complained about some man named Ben. She kept calling him an animal. Always wanting something nasty from her. That he was a goddamn degenerate truck driver who never got enough sex from her every which way.

When Debbyanne looked at Little Oscar, she smiled weakly, barely parting her blue lips, and asked, "Honey, can you get me a glass of water? And put a little whiskey in it, with some ice cubes. I feel hot. I'm so dry inside."

Little Oscar added just enough whiskey to color the water. But by the time he brought it back to her, she had forgotten what she'd asked for and the glass remained untouched on the night table by her bed.

It seemed to Little Oscar that something new was happening to his mother daily. The next day, a Thursday, during that first week of January, she developed ugly reddish-yellow abscesses on her body. They hurt her when they broke, staining the bedclothes and her pajamas. Little Oscar wiped off the pus that oozed onto her skin. And he had to wipe her mouth whenever she had a coughing and spitting spell. The sputum was a deeper-looking rust color than the previous week. He tried his best to keep her comfortable and clean, but the odor around her sometimes made him sick to his stom-

ach. He'd sneak into the bathroom and throw up without his mother hearing him.

The frustration of feeling helpless to do something to end his mother's sickness had reached an unbearable state for Little Oscar. He'd wince at the sight of her frail chest heaving for air, her nostrils sucking in, mouth open like a fish's, lips cracked and dry. He sensed she was slowly suffocating. Her features compressed into strained contortions, making her face ugly to look at.

"I'm so weak, honey," Debbyanne cried out with a breathless voice, barely audible to Little Oscar, who wanted to cry for his mother, but kept the pain inside.

Debbyanne fought for every breath she took that night and well into the morning. Then she finally admitted to Little Oscar, who had stayed at her bedside, "My chest hurts so bad, I can't stand it!" Her weakened voice was a faint squeak. "I can't get enough air. I'm suffocating. Help me, honey, help me to breathe."

Little Oscar replied, "I'm calling somebody for help, Mom. You can't take no more of this."

"Get the social worker, honey," his mother suggested.

Little Oscar left the apartment seconds later, skipping down the stairs two at a time. He didn't stop until he was in the foyer at the pay phone. He called the social worker, Mrs. Harris, at the county welfare office at ten minutes before nine that Friday morning, explaining as best he could just what his mother had been going through the past couple of weeks. Mrs. Harris replied that she'd call an emergency ambulance and that she'd come right over, hoping to get there before it arrived, since her office was closer to them than the hospital. Little Oscar thanked Mrs. Harris, relieved to hand matters over to her, then hung up and hurried upstairs.

But by the time he arrived back in his mother's bed-

room, he sensed the hopelessness of it all. So he just sat quietly by his mother and held her weak, cold hand, praying silently for a miracle, which didn't come, he soon realized. When he studied his mother's ghostly pallor, he thought he was looking at a dead woman. Her eyes were drawn deeper into her skull. The circles under them were darker with the pouchy skin sagging heavily. Red heat splotches marked her brow and cheeks, while her hand remained icy to his touch. Her blonde hair lay loose and stringy and sweat-damp on the pillow.

He watched her take a series of slow, deep, air-pulling breaths. Her flat chest heaved under the blankets like a hidden air pump. Then gasping and choking for more air, she said, "My chest hurts so bad, honey. I try, but I can't get enough air into my lungs. I'm starving for air. Help me breathe, honey, please!"

Little Oscar fought back the sick, hopeless feeling in his stomach. He wanted to cry, but didn't.

When his mother grew silent again, her eyelids closed and she became still a moment. Five seconds later her chest started working hard again, her lungs wheezing for air, lifting her body off the bed with each futile attempt to breathe.

All Little Oscar could do for his mother was to pat her hand and tell her not to worry, that the ambulance was coming and so was Mrs. Harris. That everything was going to be all right once they got her to the hospital. But he couldn't stop the knotting pain that curled his intestines into hard rubber hose unseen inside him.

After Mrs. Harris arrived, she and Little Oscar watched his mother take a noisy breath, choke on the air that didn't make it to her lungs, then gasp weakly.

Soon afterwards a rattling sound developed in her throat, followed by her chest falling slowly and then

remaining still, too still, which frightened Little Oscar. He looked up at Mrs. Harris and asked, "She isn't dying, is she?"

Mrs. Harris' young face became wide-eyed and her red-lipped mouth drooped at the corners as she replied, "I don't know, Oscar. Thank God I think I hear the ambulance's siren. Let's hope and pray they get here in time to save her. Your mother's only hope now is the hospital." Mrs. Harris placed a hand softly on Little Oscar's shoulder. He still held his mother's limp, cold blue hand. They lapsed into silence, listening for her breathing, which was faint and wheezy. Little Oscar could barely hear it. The room became a gloomy cell, with the only sounds coming from the street traffic below. The ambulance *was* the only hope for his mother. Little Oscar dropped his head against her side and let the sobs bubble up and out of him for the first time since she'd become seriously sick. Mrs. Harris patted him on the shoulder, but didn't say anything.

When they took Debbyanne out of the apartment, she had an oxygen mask strapped to her face. And by the time the ambulance arrived at the hospital, it delivered a dead body instead of a live, sick woman. Debbyanne's heart had given out on the way. The resident intern in the emergency ward tried to needle Adrenalin directly into her stilled organ, then applied electric shock to her chest.

His efforts were only temporarily successful. Debbyanne died three times that day and finally ended up in the hospital's morgue where the resident pathologist promptly performed an autopsy on her. The cause of death was determined to be cor pulmonale, heart failure as a result of lung failure.

Later it was explained to Little Oscar that had she gone to the hospital sooner, she would've had a chance to be saved, but that her staying at home for too long a time untreated, allowed the pneumonia to intensify in

her lungs and the prolonged effort to breathe eventually proved too much of a strain on her heart, which finally failed in the end.

But Little Oscar didn't care what caused his mother to die. All he knew was she was gone. The only adult he really cared about was lost to him forever. He had a deep hate and a need for revenge pumping through his own heart now for the people he felt were responsible— her parents. And he would never forgive them for what they did to his mother and him.

"What's going to happen to me now, Mrs. Harris?" Little Oscar asked as they left the hospital that evening, after the waiting ordeal ended.

"We're going to have to get you into one of the state's foster homes, Oscar. But right now you'll have to stay awhile in the county youth house. You can't stay alone in the apartment. We'll go back now to get only the necessary things for you. You can't take everything. I discussed your situation with my supervisor while we were waiting, Oscar. And we've decided to petition the state courts to have them declare you a ward of the state. The Child Welfare Services will take over your case and see to it you get a good foster home to live in."

"What about my grandparents?"

"We're going to contact them about you."

Little Oscar nodded, but he didn't want to tell Mrs. Harris he hated his grandparents and considered them responsible for his mother's death. Mrs. Harris was still part of the other world of adults. The ones he never quite trusted all the way, like with his Mom.

"What's going to happen to my mother now, Mrs. Harris?" Little Oscar asked, his voice cracking on the social worker's name.

"The city and the county will finance the burial, because of your mother's financial condition. We'll handle everything, Oscar. Don't worry. Your mother will be treated with dignity."

"I loved my mother, Mrs. Harris," Little Oscar replied, choking back a sob.

"And she loved you, I'm sure, Oscar."

Little Oscar nodded agreement. He liked Mrs. Harris better than the last fat lady they had for a social worker. He pulled up his coat collar against the biting wind. A sudden shot of pain cut into his chest as if he were being stabbed with a knife. He leaned forward; one hand pressed against his chest, the other wiping at his eyes. Mrs. Harris patted him on the shoulder, before unlocking the doors to the county-owned green sedan with the red county seal painted on both doors. Little Oscar sat on the front seat, but dreaded the return to his empty apartment. There would be so many reminders of his mother. He steeled himself against them. Because he had to act like a man now. Soon he would be on his own for the first time in his young life.

But he spent most of the trip back to the apartment wiping away tears; and he had to fight the choking anguish when he walked into the silent apartment that still smelled of his mother's sickness. He managed to just cry softly the entire time he collected his clothes and packed them in a suitcase. He didn't dare go into his mother's bedroom. It would've been too much to take. He didn't want to scream out loud or bawl like a baby in front of Mrs. Harris. It was bad enough he was crying like a sissy.

Three days later, at his mother's opened grave, it was Little Oscar, Mrs. Harris, the funeral director, his paid assistants, the grounds keepers and the paid minister in attendance. Debbyanne's final resting place would be in a public cemetery out in the suburbs, where she never got to live when alive. The irony didn't escape Little Oscar, but he said nothing to no one. He just wanted to get through the ordeal of burying his mother.

And when he looked down at the dark rectangular hole in the frozen earth, which contrasted with the white snow-covered ground and stone monuments around them, his vision blurred and he had to wipe constantly at his eyes. His mother's closed wooden casket rested a few feet away from him. He had viewed her body the night before with Mrs. Harris. No one else had been there, and there had been only one skimpy wreath of flowers on a metal stand beside the coffin. His mother had looked different in death, more like a made-up wax dummy than the real woman he remembered when alive and well before the trip to the hated farm.

The minister gave a dignified sermon about having faith in Christ and getting to heaven to spend eternity with God, then led them in a short prayer. Afterwards they took turns placing a flower on the casket and left.

Little Oscar promised himself that he'd never forget who was really putting his mother into the ground. Her parents had even begged off attending the funeral. It was one more score against them.

Later, at the cemetery gate, inside the county car with Mrs. Harris, Little Oscar turned in time to watch the grounds keepers lower his mother into the dark hole. He got that familiar pain in the chest, but he didn't cry again. Although his eyes were already burning from the enlarged red veins in the white parts, he didn't have any tears left. Just silent, bitter-tasting sorrow and hate in his heart for his grandparents.

The courts accepted Little Oscar as a ward of the state and within three weeks he was taken from the county youth house and placed in a state-supervised foster home in the northeast suburbs of Capital City. Again the irony didn't escape him, wishing he could be moving with his mother, who wanted to escape the city, but never made it when alive.

What bothered Little Oscar the most about his placement in a foster home was more strangers would now intrude into his life. He would have to cope with many new situations, including a new school setting. He hated the thoughts of it. All he wanted was his mother and their private life together. He would never forget all the wonderful times they shared and the *nice* things his mother did for him when she let him sleep with her.

But he considered this foster home placement to be just a stepping stone. During his stay in the county youth house, he daydreamed about the day the social worker would transfer him up to his grandparents' farm. He couldn't get revenge living so far away in a foster home. His first move would be to get the social worker to convince his grandparents to let him live with them.

Not that he really wanted to, but Little Oscar would do anything for his mother when she was alive, and now planned to honor her memory in death the way he knew she would be pleased. He had always been her honeybunch, and he wouldn't stop being just that. It made life worth living for him, knowing he had an ultimate goal, and was actively making plans to achieve it.

PART III

Chapter 1

"I'm gonna kill my grandparents, Spider."

"You jiving me, man, or you just plain crazy?"

"No, Spider, I'm not kidding around. Those old fools don't deserve to live, not after what they did to my mother . . . and me."

"You hate them that much?"

"They killed my mother . . . 'cause they wouldn't let us stay with them on the farm. We had to come all the way back to our apartment in Capital City that same day. We got soaked to the skin from the icy rain. Was the worst night I ever lived. I was miserable. My wet clothes made me even colder. Couldn't stop shaking. I was so tired, I could've laid down and died alongside the road. My poor mother got sick with a bad chest cold. And she brooded over what they did to us, and kept drinking and staying up late 'cause she couldn't sleep, and didn't take care of herself like she should've. Then she got pneumonia and couldn't breathe. The hospital

doctors said it strained her heart. She was a dead woman by the time the ambulance got her to the emergency ward. She was dying when they carried her out of the apartment. Had an oxygen mask strapped to her face."

"Know what you mean, man. And I sure know how you feel, too. Don't have no real parents myself. And foster parents just don't cut it for you."

"Those old fools wouldn't even come down here to see my mother buried. Their own daughter, Spider. Can't forgive them for that, neither."

"You got a powerful hate inside you. Man, I can see it deep in your eyes. It's eating up your insides."

"And it's getting worse and worse the longer I stay here."

"Yeah, ain't it like being in prison, living with the wonderful Wesleys?"

"And it looks like I'm gonna be stuck here for good, Spider, if I don't do something about it myself. Mr. Straite says my grandparents refused again to take me up there to live with them. They don't want nothing to do with me. I can't forgive them for that, neither."

"Yeah, man, you're stuck here with us till you're eighteen. Putting up with all the Wesley rules and regulations. Sometimes I think Mr. Wesley should've been a cop. And ain't Mrs. Wesley a nag? We never do nothing right to satisfy that bitch. Says this room is a pigpen, and we're a couple of slobs. She sure is a mess to get along with."

"I hate it here, Spider. And I'm not staying any longer than I have to. Can't get my revenge on those old fools, my grandparents, living down here. School's over now. And the weather's warm enough to be outdoors at night. Have to get out of here this summer. Couldn't take another year around here with the Wesleys bossing me and minding my business and blabbing to the social worker every little thing I do wrong."

"Hey, look, man, I can dig it," Spider replied. Then he leaned forward on the edge of his bed and asked, "You're not jiving me? You really got plans to take a hike?"

"Yeah, Spider, and soon."

"You are one tough little dude. But say, man, just how you going to waste your grandparents?"

"They're gonna end up like barbecued hot dogs, when I get done with them."

"Ooh, man, that's mean and nasty!"

"That's how I feel inside toward them—mean and nasty. I want to hurt those old fools, before I kill them."

"Ooh, man, that's even meaner yet. But be cool, little brother, hear? Don't let the nosy Wesleys hear you talking about busting out and wasting your grandparents. They'll blab to Mr. Straite and he'll mess up your whole murder scene. Then you'll get put away in the state hospital for being crazy, or get slapped back into the county youth house for talking mean and nasty."

"They don't worry me none, Spider. When I'm ready, I'll run away from here. The Wesleys won't know till I'm long gone, and they won't be able to do a thing about it, neither. Even if they tell the social worker, or call the cops."

"You really mean it, man, you're really busting out?"

"I'm not kidding, Spider. I hate that much."

In addition to his mushrooming hate for his grandparents, Little Oscar was secretly irritated with the state's Child Welfare Services people for placing him in a foster home that had only black children in it, since the foster parents were also black. He had never considered himself to be a Negro, despite his father having been one. Nor did he think he looked like one, despite his hair being kinky-curly, his nostrils flared, lower lip full and thick and protruding past his upper lip. For his

hair and eyebrows were blond, his eyes gray-blue and his skin tan, not brown or black. And since he was raised by his white mother, he was white in his thinking and everything else, despite their living in racially mixed urban neighborhoods. He felt no affiliation, allegiance, compassion or camaraderie with anything or anyone black. And this smoldering resentment at those responsible for placing him with the strict Wesleys added to his motivation to escape that summer when traveling would be easier.

He wouldn't miss the Wesleys, the other foster kids, even Spider. He hadn't made any close friends in the school he attended, and really didn't care to, being preoccupied with more important matters.

Little Oscar also resented being shoved up to the third-floor attic bedroom where it was cold and drafty in winter and stuffy and close in summer. He missed having a room all to himself; missed his rooftop playground, and his friends, the pigeons. The only privacy he could muster was when alone in the attic bedroom after school and Spider was outside playing basketball.

He had knowingly chanced telling Spider about his plans to run away, and to eventually kill his grandparents, after getting the news that they had refused again to take him. It had been the third inquiry by the social worker, Mr. Straite, on his behalf and at his instigation. Little Oscar had to talk out his inner anger with somebody, or he would go crazy for real. Spider was an orphan, too. He understood. Besides, after nearly six months of rooming with Spider, Little Oscar figured he knew him well enough to sense Spider wouldn't fink on him to the Wesleys or to the social worker, at least not until after he had left for good. And by that time, Little Oscar didn't care who found out, since nobody was going to stop him, just nobody.

The other thing about Spider that was convenient for Little Oscar's plans was the boy's former member-

ship in a boy scout troop, thus his being the owner of a sleeping bag, a foam rubber mattress, and a backpack— three necessary items for camping out.

Little Oscar planned to leave sooner than he had indicated to Spider. He had enough food, since he'd been stealing regularly from Mrs. Wesley's pantry and hiding the items in his suitcase in the bedroom closet. Sunday was the best day to run away. The other foster kids, including Spider, usually went to the movies; and the Wesleys took their Sunday afternoon nap religiously. But for a diversion to attract attention away from his departure, he planned to make a commotion elsewhere on the property.

As planned, Little Oscar waited until the following Sunday afternoon, July 2, 1978, when all the other foster kids in the Wesley home had scattered for the day, including Spider, who had gone to see a science fiction movie. Little Oscar had begged off, saying he had a headache. And by two in the afternoon, the Wesleys were in their bedroom, taking their siesta, as usual. The house traffic was at a standstill. Perfect for running away.

Carrying his camping gear past the Wesleys' bedroom, he could hear Mr. Wesley snoring. He walked slowly, his steps deliberate, not to creak any of the hallway floorboards and the stairs down to the first floor. In the living room he left the bedroll and backpack next to the front door.

When he left the house, Little Oscar strolled nonchalantly toward the rear of the place, as if not going anywhere in particular, but eventually made it to the old clapboard garage at the far end of the backyard. The outdated building wasn't long enough for Mr. Wesley's new 88 Oldsmobile sedan. It had been relegated to storing the lawn equipment, gardening and landscaping tools, and all the other miscellaneous accumulation not

suitable or valuable enough to store in the cellar or attic. Little Oscar had previously checked out its contents for burning possibilities; and it had plenty, from old newspapers and oily rags to cardboard boxes, plus kindling and firewood for the fireplace.

Little Oscar circled the aged frame outbuilding and climbed in through the rear window, having left it open the night before. The stuffy warm garage smelled of the earth floor, musty rags and dry newspapers, plus the distinct odor of gasoline emanating from the lawn mower. Getting right to work, he emptied and stacked a number of cardboard containers against the corner between the back and side walls. Then he crumpled newspapers around the boxes, finally pouring the last of the gasoline from a two-gallon metal can onto the makeshift cardboard pyramid. The cloying sweet smell of gasoline filled the garage. Sweat beads formed on Little Oscar's forehead. Damp spots darkened his red polo shirt.

But after he lit the first match, it was worth all the effort, watching the orange-yellow flame take hold and spread over the paper, tonguing its way up the cardboard boxes. He quickly tossed on a handful of dry wood kindling. Soon his entire paper and wood pile was in flames. When it got too smoky, Little Oscar bailed out the open rear window. He used a hedge row for cover and made it to a neighboring wooded lot unseen. Thirty seconds later he was out front of the Wesley home mounting the porch, coming in as if from playing outdoors, just like at any other time.

The street was empty of people on that quiet Sunday afternoon, and Little Oscar knew he wouldn't be spotted coming back out of the house so soon afterwards. He hastily donned the backpack once in the living room, then picked up the bedroll, and was stepping back down the front porch in less than a minute. His pace was brisk, as if on a hike. But he didn't have to

worry, no one was in sight. It had been a *piece of cake* setting the fire, and then running away from the Wesley home. He felt it was a good omen, everything was going his way.

He disregarded the pack's weight and pull of the canvas straps against his narrow shoulders, while he kept changing arms to carry the bedroll. But he never stopped walking, and even kicked up the pace when he made the first turn and headed directly away from the street that the Wesleys' home was located on. His course led him to a less-developed section of few houses and more brush- and tree-covered lots. He was three blocks away when he took his first break to catch his breath, stopping under a big shade tree, sitting for a brief moment to rest and to listen.

He didn't have to wait long. The volunteer fire company's whooping alarm could be heard for miles around. Then the clang of the fire truck's bell sounded. He even detected distant shouting voices and excited barking dogs. The fire was causing the commotion he wanted. He wouldn't be missed with all that to occupy the Wesleys' attention. His first fire was a success in the making. He wished he could be there to enjoy it, and watch the nervous Mrs. Wesley get hysterical and faint.

"I'm on my way for real now, Mom," Little Oscar said aloud to the cool wooded surroundings, looking up through the leafy tree branches at the blue sky above him. He was sure his mother was up there looking down on him, despite having seen the cemetery men lowering her into the ground. He wanted to believe the minister about going to heaven and being with Jesus— he really did.

He sighed and shrugged unconsciously, then picked up his gear and headed out of the shaded woods and into an adjacent sun-warmed open field that had rows

of growing cornstalks about a foot and a half high. It looked like a low, wavy sea of green spread out before him.

Little Oscar skirted its edge and got to the road that would take him north and eventually out of the township and the county. And once on the state highway, he hoped to get a couple of hitches, and make it to his grandparents' farm in a day's traveling time. But he knew he'd have to watch out for police cars. If they spotted a kid his age hitchhiking, they'd stop and start asking questions that he didn't want to answer.

"I'm on my way, Mom," Little Oscar said aloud again with a clipped voice from between tight lips, repeating it several times.

While he walked away from the distant-sounding confusion, Little Oscar pictured in his mind the Wesleys, their Sunday nap disturbed, running around like frightened chickens, every which way, trying to save their stupid garage. It brought a snicker or two out of him. And when he thought of Spider discovering the missing camping gear, Little Oscar shrugged unconsciously again and silently hoped his foster brother would understand enough not to fault him for it. But the Wesleys had insurance, they'd recover their loss. As to how they felt about him, he didn't care if they faulted him for what he'd done. The Wesleys, their property, Spider, his camping equipment, were just stepping stones to get him on his way back to *the farm.*

Once there he'd do the things necessary to accomplish his second goal—the final one. As for later, peering into the vague future, he could only let happen whatever was going to happen to him. Little Oscar couldn't plan in his mind any further than getting revenge for his mother and himself. Because all he really cared about right then was to please his mother, accomplishing what she had wanted to do herself, but

couldn't. He believed that she'd know he'd done it for her, wherever she was up in heaven, because the minister said she'd be spending eternity with sweet Jesus, where all true believers would be someday after they died. He hoped to join his mother when it came his turn to die. For he truly believed in Jesus. His mother used to read to him from the Bible sometimes on Sunday, whenever she was in a religious mood. She used to say it was just as good as going to church. He liked to listen to the words, picturing the biblical scenes in his head. He liked everything his mother ever did for him.

When he thought about the possibility of someday joining his mother up in heaven, as the minister had said over and over at the cemetery, he knew then that he wasn't afraid to die. He missed his mother that much.

It was dusk when Little Oscar made it to the township park, his planned night resting stop, after having walked across fields and alongside the roads, always heading north, following his township road map closely. It had scaled some three miles on paper, but seemed more like twenty to his tired feet. Having been to the park before, he knew just where to go to get the protective cover of a large grouping of blue spruce trees that hugged the park ground low to the grass. It offered the best overnight security.

Once inside the resin-scented spruce trees, he used his flashlight to help him make up a bed of dry brown needle droppings, then laid his foam rubber mat on it and the sleeping bag on top of the mat. Finally ready for his supper, he sat on his bedding and stretched out tired legs and feet.

Supper consisted of a can of vegetable soup, some crackers, and a can of root beer soda, all stolen from the

Wesleys, including the can opener and the spoon he used to eat with.

As it got darker inside the copse of fragrant spruce trees, the steady grinding and buzzing of insects surrounded him. He heard a moving car on a nearby road, and watched an airplane's wing and tail lights move across the dark sky above him, its motor a low humming sound.

When he finished eating, he took off his tube socks and sneakers, airing his sweat-damp feet a moment, before crawling into the sleeping bag. To stretch out and to rest on his back was pure luxury for him. He was alone at last, the first time since his mother died. His mind wandered from thoughts about the Wesleys and Spider to about his mother and all the good times they spent together, playing games and talking, nothing special, just enjoying each other's company.

Soon his eyes grew wet. He didn't bother to wipe them, letting the tears dribble down his temples, dampening the sleeping bag's quilted cotton material under him. He lay with blurry wet eyes, hands clasped tightly behind his neck, elbows flared outward, for uncounted minutes as the darkness engulfed him, its cool air refreshing his flushed cheeks. Then during a momentary lull from the insect noise, Little Oscar heard himself say aloud into the sudden quiet, "I love you, Mom. I miss you, too." The tears flowed harder, but he didn't wipe them.

Chapter 2

It started to rain just before Little Oscar got his first ride. Big wet drops pelted him roughly from out of swiftly moving dark gray clouds, slapping hard against his head, shoulders and arms. The gusting wind blew road dirt and paper litter around his sneakers. He watched a flock of starlings take refuge in a tree across the highway, its branches shaking and weaving in the blustery wind.

Little Oscar draped the rolled sleeping bag and foam rubber mat over his head and continued thumbing for a ride. His red cotton polo shirt became soaked by the time a sleek dark blue sedan with a white vinyl top angled sharply over to the asphalt-paved shoulder, stopping fifty feet up the highway from him. He hustled over to it, opened the wide heavy door and peered inside.

"Hi, hop in," the driver said in a friendly soprano voice.

"How far north you heading?" Little Oscar asked, studying the driver's round-cheeked tanned face.

"As far as the interstate highway." The man's broad smile curled upward under a long hooked nose and close-set, dark-pupiled eyes.

"That's good enough for a first ride, I guess," Little Oscar said, "to get me out of the rain." He sat on the light blue vinyl front seat, piling his bedroll and backpack on the floor between his legs. From inside the car, he noticed the bald man's stomach nearly touched the steering wheel. His flowery print shirt was open down to his trousers. A gold medallion hung around his fat neck on a gold chain, dangling in a patch of curly black hair between flat male breasts.

The long, fancy-looking car was doing sixty in seconds once back onto the highway, when the driver said, "I'm Elliot. My friends call me Ellie."

"I'm Oscar."

"You're awfully young to be out on the highway hitchhiking. You aren't running away, are you?"

"No, not me! I'm just heading home to my grandparents' farm for the summer. After my mother died in January, I had to live with my aunt back in the suburbs. But my aunt don't have much money. She couldn't afford to buy me a bus ticket. So I'm hitchhiking." Little Oscar studied the stranger for a moment. Did he believe the story? It was the first time he tried it out, figuring he'd get asked about his reasons for hitchhiking, everytime he got picked up.

"Sorry to hear about your mother, Oscar. But I couldn't help wondering, since you do look awfully young to be traveling alone."

"I'm older than I look, and smarter, too."

Ellie laughed briefly, then smiled thinly, his thick lips curling more than spreading. After staring intently at Little Oscar, he added "You're a very attractive young man."

Little Oscar didn't like the leer aimed at him from under those bushy black eyebrows. Nor did he like the voice tone, and the ever-present soprano lilt. But he couldn't pinpoint why. This man was not like the men who had been his mother's boyfriends. So he remained silent and stared at the passing scenery of cultivated fields and farm buildings and an occasional roadside fruit stand or eating place.

A couple of miles of concrete highway passed swiftly under them, when the man asked, "Are you camping out at night?" while glancing downward at the sleeping bag roll and backpack between Little Oscar's legs.

"Yes," Little Oscar replied, pulling the gear closer to him. And when he took a deep breath, he could smell Ellie's perfumy body cologne. It reminded him of his mother's favorite scent.

"Do you like that sort of thing, Oscar?"

"It's okay."

"Aren't you afraid of snakes, or wild animals at night?"

"I don't think about that. But I'll be careful where I walk, or sleep."

"Would you like to sleep indoors, tonight?"

"Might—where?"

"We could stop at a motel. I'll pay for the room. This way you'll have a chance to take a shower and sleep in a nice soft bed. That sleeping bag on the ground can't be comfortable."

"Sounds okay to me."

"Good, then we'll get a room and have a very nice time together. We could even stop for a meal, before we get the room. I'll treat, of course."

Ellie's voice continued to bother Little Oscar. Its lilting quality wasn't natural-sounding to him. He was used to the gruff kind of men who had kept company with his mother. And those leering, bushy eyebrows on the man's wide-cheeked face looked out of place under a

bald head. Then later during a silent moment, Ellie reached over and placed his manicured, fleshy-fingered hand on Little Oscar's knee, gradually sliding it downward along his thigh, stopping to rest at the fly of his still damp jeans.

"We're going to get along wonderfully, aren't we, Oscar?" Ellie said in his high, fluttering voice.

Again Little Oscar didn't reply, nor did he acknowledge the man's soft hand on his leg, which Ellie soon took away, returning it to the steering wheel. After nearly a mile of silence, Ellie said, "There's a service station up ahead. I have to stop and get gas. The gauge is almost on empty. Besides, I have to make a pit stop. You know, use the lavatory. Do you, Oscar? We could use it together."

"No, I'm okay," Little Oscar replied. "I'll just stay in the car and wait for you."

"All right, Oscar, I won't be long. You can keep an eye on things, while I'm indisposed." Ellie laughed wetly, the corners of his damp mouth curling up under his big, dipping nose.

Little Oscar waited until Ellie got out of sight, before he got out of the car. Ignoring the attendant's quizzical stare, he ran up the roadway about a hundred feet and turned into the first wooded grove he came to, penetrating deep enough to keep from being seen by Ellie. He sat against a tree and rested, waiting until enough time had passed before walking back toward the highway, figuring Ellie would be heading north by then, looking for some other hitchhiker to keep him company that night. At least Little Oscar knew it wasn't going to be him. No way was he sleeping with a strange-acting man. He still remembered what Buck had tried to do to him.

It had started to rain again by the time Little Oscar made it back to the highway. But he ignored the watery

drops that landed on him, walking along the grassy edge of the road's shoulder with his arm stuck out and thumb raised whenever a car or truck approached him.

He managed only one more short-distanced ride in an hour of walking and hitchhiking, when he spotted a southbound state police car suddenly slow down and swing over to make a U-turn at the grass median barrier a few hundred feet past him, with the policeman inside staring his way.

Little Oscar exited quickly into the adjacent thick undergrowth and trees. He didn't stop running until he came to a planted field, with farm buildings a thousand feet off in the distance. He dropped his bedroll and backpack on the ground between the trees to his back and the first row of low-lying green plants, which he couldn't identify, at his feet. Then he sat beside his gear and worked to get back his breath, his chest heaving, lungs aching for air. He wondered if the police would be looking for him from now on, and decided to remain where he was and not chance going back to the highway until the next morning.

He opened a can of pork and beans and ate them slowly, along with a couple of crackers and cookies for dessert, drinking his last can of root beer to wash it all down, enjoying the tepid, sweet-tasting soda to the last mouthful. Afterwards he made up his bed and sat on it.

In a short while, he became bored with just sitting and staring at the rural scene before him, and with listening to the birds flying overhead, and with swatting flies off his face and head. He decided to explore the edge of the field, walking crouched to keep from being seen. It was fun. He covered a quarter mile one way, then retraced his steps back to his campsite, and did the same thing in the other direction. Once settled again, he ate a couple more cookies, while listening to dogs barking and voices coming from near the farm buildings. When it grew quiet again, he relaxed and

munched slowly on one more sugary-tasting cookie.

An hour later, Little Oscar zipped himself into his sleeping bag. And with his hands clasped under his head, staring up at the early twinkling stars in the clear darkening sky, he whispered aloud, "Don't you worry, Mom, I'm gonna make it."

"Hey—wake up, sleepyhead!" a gruff voice commanded.

A hard object pushed against his leg inside the sleeping bag, while a flashlight's cutting brightness blinded him. Little Oscar couldn't see beyond the light. He sat up, shielding his eyes with a forearm.

"Hold back the dogs, son," the harsh-sounding voice said from the darkness.

Little Oscar could hear the dogs straining on their leashes, but he couldn't see them.

"At least till we find out what this trespasser's doing on our land," the voice said in a mocking tone. "We saw you, boy, walking along the edge of the field. You a runaway?"

Little Oscar unzippered the sleeping bag and slid out. He couldn't see who was behind the flashlight, its constant glare aimed into his eyes. "Just getting some sleep," he replied. "I wasn't doing nothing else." Little Oscar guarded his eyes with a flat palm and extended fingers. The light hurt his eyes. "I don't want any trouble. I'm leaving right now." He rolled up his sleeping bag and mat and hurriedly tied them, strapped on his backpack, then picked up the bedroll and stood up. But he waited for his cue to leave, still keeping his distance from the unseen dogs that whined to get at him from out there in the threatening darkness.

"Hold on, boy. Maybe the state police should know about you."

"Why? I didn't steal nothing. I'm just heading north to go live with my grandparents for the summer. They

got a farm up north from here. I was living with an aunt down in Capital City. She knows all about me traveling alone. She couldn't give me any money to take the bus. So I'm hitchhiking, and camping out, till I get there."

"Gutsy little guy, ain't he?" the shadowy older man said to his son, who just snickered somewhere in the dark, but didn't reply.

Little Oscar continued to squint in the glare of the flashlight, while the bedroll grew heavier in his grasp.

"Think we should let him go, son?" The voice was taunting. "If he gets off our property in one minute?"

Again there wasn't any reply, just snickering from the son.

"You'd better get moving, boy, and don't trespass on this property again, or we'll turn the dogs loose on you. They'll make your little ass feel like hamburger."

The unseen son laughed out loud.

"I'm leaving," Little Oscar replied, turning abruptly and walking quickly into the brush and trees behind him. He used his forearm to ward off the low-lying tree branches and bushes, increasing his walking pace the deeper he penetrated the woods. The distant sounds of fast-moving trucks guided him toward the highway, where he gladly spent the rest of the night in his sleeping bag on the edge of its grassy shoulder just twenty-five feet from the concrete paving. Morning couldn't come fast enough for him.

It was three short rides of a couple miles each, and a lot of walking later, when he stopped for lunch, staying hidden off the highway; then he spotted two state police cars, one cruising slowly north, the other south. Were they looking for him? Allowing for that possibility, he took a longer-than-usual lunch break, before venturing out to try his thumb at hitchhiking again. And to his pleasant surprise, within a short time, a boxy-looking,

rusting gray vehicle pulled over to the shoulder up from him and he ran to it. When he opened the door opposite the driver, Little Oscar said, "I'm heading north to where Creek Road meets the main highway."

"We're heading up that way a few miles, little brother. It'll help you get closer to your destination. Get in." The driver's voice was friendly, and he had a white terry cloth headband holding back long black hair that covered his ears and brushed against his shoulders.

Little Oscar climbed in and sat next to the driver. The other passengers included a young woman with long straight brown hair holding a baby on her lap, sitting directly behind the driver. Another young woman sat beside her. She looked like the twin of the woman holding the baby. They smiled a welcome at him; and he noticed they wore white tee shirts without bras underneath, their nipples obvious under the thin cotton material.

Later, after rattling steadily along, the girl behind him said, "You look real young, little brother. You busting out from somewhere?"

"Yeah, he does look young," the driver said. "You on the road for kicks, or on purpose?"

Little Oscar started to mumble a noncommittal reply, then sensing he could tell these young people *almost* the truth, he said, "Couldn't take anymore shit from my stiff foster parents. I'm heading up north to get back with my grandparents. They got a nice farm. So I'm gonna stay with them for the summer."

"That's cool, little brother," the driver said, grinning and revealing a missing side tooth. "At least you're doing your own thing. Stick with us. Every mile closer counts, right, girls?"

"Why not? I think he's cute, don't you, Melissa?" the girl with the baby asked her look-alike.

"Sexy cute, Deni. And I love his curly hair. Can I touch it, little brother?" Melissa asked Little Oscar,

who giggled his approval as she placed a thin, soft hand with dirty fingernails on his head, gently stroking his kinky-curly blond hair. Then she slid her hand down his neck and touched briefly at his ear before taking her hand away.

After a few minutes of silence, the girl with the baby suggested, "Why don't we take our new friend to the farmhouse, so he can eat with us? Would you like an all-vegetable supper, little brother? It's healthy, natural food and good for you. Better than the Fourth of July picnic junk food everybody's eating today."

"I'm hungry. I could eat anything," Little Oscar replied, hoping to save on his food supply. "How far off the highway is your farmhouse?"

"Just a half mile or so, little brother," the driver said.

Little Oscar nodded his approval and relaxed, sitting back on the worn vinyl seat with the seams splitting, anticipating something to drink as well as eat, since his throat was as dry as dusty burlap.

It was a fifteen minute interval of slow, tedious, muffler-popping driving up and down a number of lengthy hills, before they turned off into a dirt and stone driveway and bumped along over the potholes until they came to a dilapidated farmhouse and equally depressed outbuildings. Holes and missing siding marked leaning walls. Roofs sagged precariously above their supports. They parked between the farmhouse and an open shed garage with a vintage VW bug sedan inside supported on jacks, its tires missing. And when they got out of the boxy vehicle, tail-wagging mongrel dogs sniffed them as they walked toward the unpainted clapboard farmhouse. Semiwild farm cats and kittens scattered out of their way.

Inside the farmhouse smelled of soiled diapers, cat and dog fur and musty furniture and rugs. A faint

punky odor hung in the stale indoor air. The screenless windows were flung open, letting in flies and the equally sultry humid air from outside. In the kitchen, Little Oscar drank cool well water from an unwashed glass, then adjourned to the living room and sat on a nap-worn sofa. The aged furniture creaked under his light weight. He kept his bedroll and backpack on the floor between his legs. The pacifier-sucking baby crawled an inch at a time on the dusty, worn rug in the center of the room, trying to grab hold of a meowing kitten's tail. The driver and the two girls remained in the kitchen, preparing the mixed vegetables for supper.

When ready, they ate in the kitchen on the rickety wooden table that squeaked noisily, as if the legs were going to give way every time somebody bumped into it. Little Oscar enjoyed a glass of freshly squeezed carrot juice as well as the assortment of chopped, diced and cut raw vegetables and fruit on his plate, all grown in the garden and orchard behind the farmhouse. He had seconds on everything, despite tired jaws from all the steady, noisy chewing.

After supper they trooped into an adjacent room that had two wide mattresses on the bare wood floor, with some wrinkled blankets tossed nearby.

When they settled on the stripped, stained mattresses, the driver, still wearing his soiled white headband, lit up an oval-shaped, brown paper-covered cigarette and inhaled off it deeply, holding the smoke in his lungs an extra beat before exhaling. Then he passed it to Deni, who did likewise. She passed it to Melissa, who sucked eagerly on the wet end and held the smoke an extra count also, before breathing it out into the warm bedroom. Melissa passed it to Little Oscar, who followed their lead and giggled at the results.

"Take another hit off the joint, little brother, it'll get you up faster. Make you feel loose. You'll groove bet-

ter," the driver said to Little Oscar, who nodded and sucked on the wet end of the makeshift cigarette again.

A second joint was lit and passed around. And in a short while they were all grinning sheepishly with heavy, drooping eyelids. The whites of their eyes reddened noticeably with the tiny swollen veins showing.

Little Oscar recognized the punky odor in the bedroom from earlier, when he had first entered the farmhouse.

Then the driver passed around a bottle of red wine. They sipped from the bottle until it was empty.

Little Oscar did grow loose and relaxed, leaning back on the mattress full length, staring up at the dark ceiling, which seemed so far away from him that he'd need a twenty-foot ladder to climb up and touch the faded wallpaper.

The driver lit two candles, which soon gave off a mixed paraffin and incense odor.

After a silent interlude, Deni and Melissa started whispering to each other and ended up laughing and leering with their big brown eyes rolling, full-lipped mouths grinning widely.

Melissa was the first one to take off her tee shirt and jeans. She was naked instantly, not wearing any underwear. Her large, white-skinned breasts stuck out firmly with jutting, round, darker-skinned nipples. She had a brownish-black clump of hair between her tanned thighs and white-skinned pelvis and hips.

Deni stripped off her dirty painter pants and white tee shirt and was naked immediately, also. She had the same white- and tan-striped look as Melissa, equally large breasts with big, silver dollar-size nipples. Her crotch was dark-haired and just as bushy-looking.

Little Oscar marveled at their dark patches of hair. His mother's had been lighter, more brownish, and not so hairy.

The driver shed his ragged-edged cut-offs and wrinkled, holey tee shirt and was naked like the girls in seconds, except for his headband. The hair on his flat chest, skinny legs and flopping genitals was as black as his head.

"How about you, little brother, aren't you going to take your clothes off?" Melissa asked Little Oscar.

"Oh, come on, get naked. It'll make you free," Deni added.

"Yeah, little brother, you're one of the gang now," the driver said.

Then all three of them came laughingly over to where Little Oscar lay and gently, but firmly, peeled off his clothes. He was naked with exposed hairless genitals in less than a minute. His jeans, sneakers, polo shirt, socks and urine-stained Jockey shorts were in disarray on the dusty floor next to the mattress. And to his own surprise, he didn't resist them.

"Ooh, isn't his little cock cute, Deni? And his balls feel like soft marbles."

"Not a feather on him, huh, girls?" the driver said.

"Let me get a feel in, too," Deni said.

Little Oscar giggled at their fondling of his hairless genitals.

"I'll bet that cute little cock even tastes good."

"Don't eat it all up, Melissa, save some for me."

"How about mine, girls, nobody wants to chew on it?" the driver asked, with a mock hurt tone to his voice.

Deni and Melissa took turns stroking and performing orally on Little Oscar's short upright penis and the driver's larger, stiff member, also, before they took turns mounting them in ladies delight fashion, with Little Oscar and the driver lying on their backs on the multistained bare mattresses. They undulated hips and pelvises over the clitoris-massaging penises inside them, and didn't stop till each had a muscle-

contracting, lip-biting, moaning orgasm, taking shift turns on Little Oscar and the driver. They managed two satisfying climaxes each for their efforts.

The sudden physical intimacy with Deni and Melissa brought back similar intimate scenes with his mother. Little Oscar closed his eyes and relived them even more vividly. But whenever he opened his eyes and saw either of the girls on top of him, he experienced a twinge of guilt. He secretly hoped his mother wasn't seeing him right then. But he proudly remembered that he had satisfied her just like those bigger, stronger men used to. She had always called him her honeybunch and her best lover.

He closed his eyes again and let the pleasures of the moment continue to help him relive pleasures of the past. His head and body floated and tingled outwardly to his fingertips and toes. He giggled his delight.

Before they bedded down for the night, with Deni, Melissa, the baby and the driver staying in the downstairs bedroom, and Little Oscar adjourning to the living room to set up his bedding, they had stated their intentions of trying the same fun and games routine the next evening. And that Little Oscar should spend another full day and night with them. He had smiled, giggled, but only shrugged his shoulders, without replying verbally and committing any of his future time and services.

Little Oscar slept fitfully, dozing off for only minutes at a time. When he spotted the first crack of light through the living room window, he got up and dressed quickly, then gathered his gear and made ready for traveling.

Out in the morning dampness, which was neither cold nor warm, the dogs sniffed his jeans and sneakers and the same cats and kittens scattered before him as he made his silent way down the bumpy stone and dirt

driveway, stepping around and over stagnant puddles of muddy water, heading briskly toward the highway. The fresh air was invigorating after the stale odors in the farmhouse from the punky-smelling cigarettes, their wine breath, body armpits, wet crotches and stinky feet. He couldn't get enough of it into his lungs.

It was fully daylight by the time he made it to the highway and immediately began thumbing for a ride and walking north in order to get distance between him and those crazy young people. He got his first ride from a dump truck driver hauling stone, and was relieved to be on his way again after yet another delay. He had a promise to keep to his mother, and nothing was going to stop him from keeping it—nothing.

Later, toward evening, after another frustrating day of short rides, ducking state police cars and lots of walking, then eating the last of his food in the backpack, he approached a fruit stand owner and asked if he could help with chores in return for some fruit to eat. But the owner refused him, without apology. Little Oscar didn't comment or make any rebuttal, he simply turned and walked silently away, stopping a hundred feet north of the stand, where he dropped his gear by a tree at the edge of the grassy shoulder. He waited for the next car to pull up to the stand, before walking back to wait in the nearby concealing brush, while the owner became occupied in serving the customer. Like an infantryman in battle, he crawled the ten feet to the nearest basket of peaches, dragging his empty backpack with him, where he grabbed handfuls of ripe peaches and stuffed it to capacity.

But when he heard the customer say out loud to the owner, "Hey, that kid's robbing peaches off you," Little Oscar jumped to his feet and ran a slanted course into the nearest brush and trees, penetrating the cover about four hundred feet, before stopping and resting against a tree trunk; there he ate slowly, savoring each

peach as if it would be his last, licking the sweet-tasting juice off his dirty fingers.

It was over an hour later, with the evening darkening fast, when he got up and followed the sounds of the passing trucks and cars and found the highway again near the fruit stand. He quickly located the tree where his bedroll waited and moved up the roadway about a quarter mile, finally entering a piney grove of scented evergreen trees to bed down for the remainder of the night a hundred feet from the highway. It had been one more delay in a long line of delays, but he had eaten and he was sure he'd make Creek Road the next day. His road map indicated he was only a couple of miles away. And he silently assured his mother that he'd make it to the farm the next day, being so close, before dropping off to sleep.

It was the last leg on that surprisingly long trip. The same one that he and his mother had done in less than twenty-four hours that miserably wet night over six months ago. But they had gotten quicker rides from van drivers and two long rides from truckers for services rendered by his mother. One trucker had sent him into a diner to get coffee, while his mother stayed behind in the tractor. Little Oscar knew what they were going to do. It had been worth it, getting the second trucker to go twenty miles out of his way to take them into Capital City that night in the rain. The other driver had his mother service him orally while driving, with Little Oscar lying on the bunk behind them. Now the ninety odd miles to *the farm* had taken him four days already, because of the short rides and the delays. And Creek Road was a five-mile stretch itself to cover. Rides would be scarce. It would probably be hiking all the way.

The next morning he was up at dawn, walking and thumbing early, but without any luck in getting a ride.

He ended up walking the last three miles to Creek Road; and when he finally stared down its steeply crowned black asphalt surface, Little Oscar told himself, "Just five more miles, don't give up now." A sudden tightness choked off the air in his throat and tears filled his eyes. "I'm almost back there, Mom," he said aloud. "You just got to wait a little bit longer, and you'll get your wish. I promised you that before you died. You didn't hear me. But I promised."

Chapter 3

Little Oscar's social worker, Carl Straite, steered the black state-owned sedan up onto the stone and dirt driveway of the Rocklands' farm. He'd been there before, having made three previous trips in Little Oscar's behalf, attempting to persuade the Rocklands to house the boy with them. His original impression of the farm had been negative, and the place looked more depressed and seedier with each subsequent visit. But now, after only a month, the farm was barely one step above a rural ghetto. Back in the spring, he had wondered why the kid had wanted to live there, especially with a grouch like Morley Rockland. Straite had assumed then that his intent was sincere, wanting to live with relatives, rather than with strangers in a foster home.

Straite wasn't looking forward to talking to the Rocklands again, even though his visit wasn't to try to sell them the idea of having Oscar live with them, and how pleased it would make one little boy. The soft-sell approach had never dented the old man's armor, with

his refusing adamantly all three times. And since Oscar was a ward of the state, the agency couldn't force the move to the grandparents' home.

The Rocklands weren't his favorite kind of people. Morley Rockland had literally growled his negative reply like a famished bear fresh out of hibernation during the third and final entreaty to take Oscar with them. He remembered the old man's disposition had gotten worse with each successive approach on the subject. Straite could think of a hundred things he'd rather be doing.

The hot, humid summer weather wasn't exactly ideal for traveling. Not having air conditioning in the agency's Ford, Straite had to drive with the windows open. After ninety miles of wind and road dust, his face was as gritty as sand and his hair resembled a rag mop. His skin was covered with a film of sweat. It was going to be a miserable afternoon in more ways than one.

Before he got out of the car, he rebuttoned his shirt collar, tightened his blue- and red-striped tie, and recombed his hair, using the rearview mirror for guidance, making sure every strand of his neck-length chestnut-brown hair was in place. Once out of the car, he donned his blue polyester and cotton summer-weight suit jacket and trudged up the front porch steps, which creaked disconcertingly under his two-hundred-pound bulk.

It was obvious to him now just why Oscar wanted to live on the Rockland farm. The kid had a scheme in the back of his devious little mind. And he had used his social worker as diplomat and courier to *sell* the Rocklands, promoting his intentions, which, ironically, had failed. Then he had to resort to extreme measures, like running away to get up there to the Rockland farm.

Straite rotated his head slowly back and forth. What the hell was he doing in social work anyway? Maybe he should have gone into sales, or teaching?

Anything that wasn't as depressing, dealing with losers all the time. Social work was a woman's field anyway. What the hell was he doing trying to crack their domain? Maybe he should have gone back to work in the construction business, like before his army days and during his college summer vacations? Straite rotated his head again, but more slowly the second time. Even that kind of masculine work had lost its appeal to him, and he knew it. Was his life and career going nowhere fast? It made him depressed to think about it.

Steeped in these moody thoughts, he knuckled the wooden front door. Its gray paint flaked off on his knuckles from the effort. When it was finally flung open, Morley Rockland stood before him in the open doorway, squinting owlishly behind thick-lensed bifocals. He looked more like an obstacle than a greeter.

"Oh, it's you again. Look, Straite, don't even ask. The answer's no, before you start yapping," Morley Rockland said, his voice gravelly, upper lip lifting like a snarling junkyard dog.

"You can relax, Mr. Rockland," Straite began, keeping his voice low and modulated, "I'm not here to ask you and your wife to take Oscar to live with you."

"Then why the hell are you here?"

"Your grandson's run away."

"That's none of my bother, now is it, Straite? You know I never recognized him legally as my grandson. He's still an illegitimate nigger bastard in my book. He'll never be my grandson—never!"

"As it happens, it just may be a bother to you, Mr. Rockland. May I come in and explain?"

"There's no use of you coming in the house. We can talk just as well right here. Ain't that right, Sarah?"

Sarah Rockland had lumbered heavily up to the doorway on swollen legs, looking every day of her age, dressed in her usual faded gray apron over a shapeless housedress, exhibiting a lumpy physique with no shape

163

or form, just mass. She stood next to her husband, blinking behind bifocals, her thinning white hair hanging loosely at her temples. After an awkward moment of silence, she asked, "What's the matter now?" Her voice came out in a nasal whine.

"Just some nonsense about Debbyanne's nigger bastard. Nothing for us to worry about. Right, Straite?"

"I think there is something to be concerned about, Mr. Rockland. Oscar made some threatening statements concerning you and your wife. He told his roommate about his intentions. And we have reason to believe he means to carry them out."

"What can that little squirt do to us?" Morley Rockland replied, laughing hoarsely, bending forward from the effort. Then after a coughing spell, he straightened himself and added, "I'll step on the smart ass like an ant, if he comes up here acting wise and threatening us."

"Oscar told his roommate he was going to run away, Mr. Rockland. And he did just that. He also told the boy he intended to kill his grandparents, because of what they did to his mother and him."

"Oh, he does, does he? That pip-squeak is all talk, Straite."

"He blames you two for killing his mother, by not taking them in last December, and making them go back to the city in bad weather, with his mother getting sick, then eventually dying. He's firmly convinced that you two caused her death, and he means to get revenge. He sees you two as villains, because in his mind, you destroyed his world, when you caused his mother to get sick and die."

"That's nonsense, Straite."

"But to Oscar it isn't, Mr. Rockland. It's reality. And I believe he really intends to try and kill you two. He hates you that much. I think his warped hatred has

grown to enormous proportions. We can't, or we shouldn't, dismiss his desire for revenge as youthful fantasy. From what his roommate said, Oscar feels much too strongly against both of you. I wouldn't take his threats lightly."

"How does that tiny jerk intend to kill us, Straite?"

"I'm not sure. But the roommate mentioned something about his barbecuing both of you. I guess he means to burn you up. It sounds farfetched, but it's a sick boy we're dealing with."

Morley Rockland laughed hoarsely again, and had another coughing spell, then finally spit into a wrinkled checkered handkerchief, before replying, "That pint-size ape doesn't scare me none, Straite. How's he going to set fire to us? I'll squash him like a mosquito, before he gets a chance to light one match around here, right, Sarah?"

Sarah Rockland shrugged and replied, "If you say so, Dad."

"He's been seen on the road heading north just a few days ago. The state police spotted a boy hitchhiking out on the main highway some fifty miles south of here, who answered to his description. They lost sight of him when he ran into the woods. He could be anywhere now, making his way up here. We know he's heading in this direction, that's for sure. And it's obvious, Oscar's determined to accomplish just what he told his roommate he'd do. He's a strong-willed little guy. A lot more so than his size indicates. And he loved his mother more so than normal. I'm sure of that, also. Obviously, that's the main reason for his outrageous hate against both of you for destroying the only person he ever loved in his short life so far. He can't forgive you for that. In fact he'll *never* forgive you for that. That's why he wanted me to convince you to take him up here to live. It would've made it easy for him to hurt you in some way.

165

That's obvious now, after revealing his intentions to his roommate, and then actually running away from the foster home."

"Look, Straite, if that nigger shows his face around here, he'll get his ass kicked up around his shoulders. I'm still not too old to straighten him out real fast. And if he gets smart with me, I'll let my new dog make a second hole in his short black ass." Morley Rockland had another fit of hoarse, choking laughter and coughing, then straightened up and added, "Come on, Straite, I'll show you the dog. He's the meanest son-of-a-bitch I ever seen. Half shepherd and half Doberman. Got him off a neighbor of mine for twenty bucks. Can't get a meaner combination than shepherd and Doberman, right, Sarah?"

"Can't is right," Sarah Rockland replied. "That monster scares the dickens out of me," she added with a wave of the dish towel she held in her thickly veined hand, blinking her eyes rapidly behind rimless bifocals.

Morley Rockland shuffled past Straite onto the front porch, then led him down the wooden steps and back to the outbuildings, stopping near the frame packing shed that had obviously been in disuse for years. He pointed a bent, accident-shortened forefinger at the doghouse next to it.

Its hairy animal occupant came charging out at them with a bark that was more of a strung-out growl from deep in its long throat. Straite jumped back. Morley Rockland laughed and said, "Don't worry, Straite, the chain won't break." The dog had jacked itself up off its big front paws, with the attached heavy-gauge iron chain taut as a steel rod, sticking straight out from the doghouse mount. Then it paced back and forth in a semicircle, straining to get free. The narrow-mouthed head was more Doberman than shepherd, and its stocky body was more shepherd than Doberman. Inch-long wet fangs added to the menace.

"He's not only mean, he's downright nasty, Mr. Rockland," Straite said. "Those teeth look sharp enough to kill me, if he ever got a hold of my throat."

"That's why I bought him, Straite. Even the Mrs. won't go near him. I've got to feed him all the time myself, even when I'm ailing. And does he get onery, if I make him wait, and he's hungry. After he eats and calms down, I let him run around. Big dogs need plenty of exercise. Can't keep him chained up all the time. He'd get mean enough to turn on me. The Mrs. locks herself in the house when I let him run loose."

"What's the monster's name?"

"I call him Judas. Got long thin legs like a full-blooded doby. Yet, he's got a strong stocky body like a shepherd, and he runs like a deer."

"Just don't let him loose now. I believe you, Mr. Rockland," Straite replied, moving back a few feet as the dog whined and strained to get at him, practically choking itself on its collar.

Morley Rockland laughed hoarsely again, sounding as if he had a bag of loose, tumbling stones in his red-necked throat. Then he led Straite back some seventy-five feet toward the state car parked next to the farmhouse. "Don't worry about us, Straite, we'll watch out for that crazy kid. And Judas will, too. That's why I got him, because of all the burglaries around the township. Crime's moved out to the country. It's just as bad as in the cities anymore. We even got a dope problem out at the regional high school. These kids are disgusting today."

"That's surprising—and disillusioning, Mr. Rockland."

"I tell you, Straite, this country's falling apart at the seams. And you know what?—I'm glad I'm old. I won't live much longer. Won't have to see this once-fine country go to pot completely. It'll never come back, believe you me it won't. And that's a damn shame. No-

body has respect for anything anymore. Not for each other. Property. The police. Even school teachers and principals are nobodies to the school kids these days. Nothing but a bunch of animals living in this country now. They've lost touch with God. Nobody has any real belief in religion inside them anymore. Nothing but a bunch of heathens. I'm glad I won't be around come the next century. Because I've sure as hell had enough of living in this one. I can tell you that much."

Straite grunted agreement and tossed his suit jacket onto the backseat of the state car and got in behind the steering wheel. He inserted the key into the ignition, but waited for the right moment to start the motor. Morley Rockland stood nearby in his faded Farmer Brown overalls, the wide blue straps fastened over bare shoulders. Straite could see Sarah Rockland peeping at him from behind sheer summer curtains at one of the living room's side windows. "Well, Mr. Rockland," he began, "I just wanted to pass along the warning about Oscar to both of you, today. And if you do spot Oscar, don't waste your time trying to apprehend him, just call the police, and then call me. I'll come up here in a hurry. But let the authorities handle things. It'll be best for Oscar and you. The boy needs understanding and psychiatric help; that's obvious now, isn't it?"

"Psychiatric help, hell! First, I'll kick his ass, Straite, then I'll call you and the police."

"That won't be necessary, Mr. Rockland. Just call the police. Oscar's a confused, hurt boy. He needs help. He really does. And he doesn't need his rear end kicked. He's had enough rejection already at his young age."

The old man didn't reply, just made a froggy noise inside his throat, like grinding pebbles, and shook his head with quick, jerky movements. He stepped back from the car when Straite started the motor.

Straite backed the car out of the driveway and stopped at the road, waving goodbye to the elderly farmer, who waved back and approached the car. "I'm not worried, Straite, so don't you worry about us none," he hollered above the engine noise, his voice sounding like gurgling water. "We can take care of ourselves good enough. Been doing it all our lives. And my Judas'll keep an eye on things around here for us. That dog can hear a mouse run on grass. He'll warn us if that kid shows up. So don't worry about us, Straite. So long."

Straite waved again, then drove the state sedan slowly away from the Rockland farm, heading toward the Creek Road intersection. In the rearview mirror, he watched the aged farmer turn and shuffle slowly back toward the farmhouse's front porch, his posture slanted forward, more so than when walking to and from the doghouse.

The bent man's stringy white hair tossed lightly in the steady, strong breeze, resembling dry bleached straw. It was almost transparent in the glary summer sunlight.

"I did my job," Straite said aloud. "My conscience is clear. They can't say I didn't warn them. But nobody listens. I shouldn't have expected them to. Still, I warned them." He shook his head, as if it were on a rotating disc in his neck, then turned his attention back to driving, steering the car onto Creek Road. He pressed his right foot down harder on the accelerator. The sedan's hood raised slightly and shot forward faster. The wind whistled past the open windows. He wanted to get to the main highway sooner, where he could make better time, hoping to get back to the agency's office in Capital City before the five o'clock closing time and report to his female supervisor that he had done as instructed.

"My conscience is clear," he said, repeating it twice

more, sounding like a low-volume voice recording with the needle stuck in the same groove of the record, going round and round on it.

Chapter 4

Little Oscar left Creek Road and stepped carefully into the nearby brush, ever watchful for wiggly snakes as he crunched dead leaves and twigs beneath his dirty canvas sneakers. He circled a wide oak tree and used it for a privacy shield, urinating on the trunk, his yellow waste fluid splashing brightly off the grooved bark surface, darkening its porous texture in a rapidly descending trail. And when he finished, he paused an extra moment, enjoying the woodsy cooler air on his damp skin. The afternoon had grown from summer warm to summer hot. The sun and the humidity had drawn sweat beads on his skin with every step. Hiking on Creek Road's black macadam surface was like walking in a frying pan. The soles of his feet were hot and sweaty. He wasn't in a hurry to leave the natural canopy for the waiting heat and sun out on Creek Road.

He had left his bedroll in the brush just off the road, not far from where he stood. But he could still see out to the roadway, while shielded from exposure twenty feet

inside the wooded tract. He was getting good at this kind of stealth, as if he were an American Indian boy from pre-colonial times, rather than an urban child of the twentieth century.

From the angle of the sun in the sky, prior to side-tracking into the woods, he had determined the time to be around three o'clock, or maybe as late as three-thirty. He still had at least three more miles of hot walking before getting to his grandparents' farm. He was foot- and leg-tired, taking more rest stops to pull off his clammy tube socks and threadbare sneakers to air sweat-damp feet, which were smelling more like stinky Limburger cheese everyday. He couldn't remember the last time he had washed them.

But he remembered a peach orchard on the south side of Creek Road about halfway between his grand-parents' farm and the main highway. And he made a mental note to make another stop there for a quick for-aging of peaches, at least enough to fill his backpack again, after first filling his stomach. It would be enough food to get him through the day and into tomor-row. For at that stage in his plans, he shunned any thought of the day after that. Life had taken on a primi-tive immediacy. He had already lost track of the days. Whether it was Thursday or Friday, he didn't know; and when he thought about it, he didn't care. The cal-endar's march of days had lost its meaning for him, and the future had lost its vague appeal. He couldn't foresee any attraction for him beyond what he had planned for the immediate time ahead. He lived now only for realiz-ing his plans in regards to his grandparents and their farm. It was going to be the high point of his young life. As he saw it, the low point had already been reached with his mother's death; and as far as he could envision reality in his callow mind, he had nowhere to go but up since then. Up to what? He had no idea.

It was after he had shaken the last yellow drops off his penis, and had zipped up his fly, while walking toward the road again, that he heard an approaching car from the direction of his grandparents' farm. An inner sense stopped him. From the concealment of the last line of brush cover, he watched a familiar-looking official black sedan with a gold seal on the door drive rapidly up the road's incline toward where he knelt. He remembered the type of car from having ridden in them a number of times. Slouching lower behind the bush in front of him, while brushing gnats off his face, he studied the passing vehicle to determine if the driver had spotted him. But when it drove quickly by, with the driver staring straight ahead, Little Oscar was not only relieved, he was surprised at recognizing the driver as well. It was Mr. Straite. He'd know the tall man's sharply defined, pointed-nose profile anywhere, and the long brown hair blowing loosely in the wind. He also recognized his style of driving, with both hands high up on the steering wheel, leaning forward at a slight angle, looking more like a stock car driver on a dirt racetrack than a social worker in a state car on a paved country road.

Little Oscar watched the low-slung, boxy-looking car disappear over and down the hilly incline to his left in the direction of the main highway. Mr. Straite was driving fast, obviously in a hurry to get back to Capital City. Little Oscar considered himself lucky that he hadn't been out on the road. He would've been seen easily. He was glad he had followed his impulse to stay put. To get caught, after getting so far, was something he didn't want to think about; not after struggling for almost a week and getting so close to his objective, with only a couple-three more hours of hiking to go.

He considered it a good omen, spotting Mr. Straite without the social worker seeing him. Now he was sure

the state police were alerted, and had been out looking for him. And thinking back, he realized his decision to run and hide deep in the woods by that farm was the right one. Plus seeing Mr. Straite coming back from his grandparents' farm was proof enough that he must've visited them. He wondered what Mr. Straite had told them. Did Spider tell the social worker about his intentions of killing his grandparents? Did Mr. Straite warn his grandparents about it? Little Oscar had to assume that he did just that, after seeing him tearing up Creek Road like a race car driver.

Maybe it hadn't been smart telling Spider about his plans. Yet he had to tell somebody about the hurt feelings inside him, after all the rejections by his grandparents. The total hurt against his mother and himself was too deep and too sharply cutting, like a stabbing butcher's knife, to keep it from coming to the surface. He had to get the worst part out into the open, so that he could hear it said aloud, and then see the wide-eyed shock on Spider's lean, bony face.

But at least now he was in a position of knowledge. He knew now that his grandparents would be wary, looking out for his approach to their farm. He would have to be even more cagey in order to get on their farm without them knowing he was there, if he was to succeed and please his mother up in heaven, and himself down on earth. Once on the farm undetected, he'd need only a day to organize himself; and then do the torching quickly after that, like the next day.

"Tomorrow, Mom," Little Oscar mumbled, "it's gonna happen tomorrow, I promise." And the word—tomorrow—rang like a dull-sounding bell in his head. He could see the letters TOMORROW in front of his eyes as if printed on paper. Only a day's more time and it would be all over for them. He enjoyed the thought, picturing the flames climbing in their orangy-red brightness up the faded gray clapboard sides of the

farmhouse, resembling the fires of hell, climbing higher and higher up those dried-out wooden walls. It was going to be something to behold, like out of a scary movie.

After he returned to the sun-baked macadam of Creek Road, Little Oscar said aloud, "I'm almost there, Mom. Didn't I promise you I'd make it?" A smile spread his dry, cracked lips. "See, you got nothing to worry about. Because nobody's stopping me. Not Mr. Straite. Not the cops. Nobody." Then he headed briskly toward the hilly eastern horizon, swatting at the busy gnats that crawled into his nostrils, open mouth and eyes. Flies buzzed his head like dive bombers. But he kept moving at a good pace, with the bulky bedroll under his right arm and the backpack tugging loosely at his shoulders.

"Here we go, Judas, boy, got a nice big dish of your favorite dog food and table scraps for you," Morley Rockland said in his hoarse voice that sounded as if he had a mouthful of stones.

Judas jumped and tugged at his hated chain, then pounced on the heaping plate of food placed before him, devouring it in less than a minute. Morley Rockland chuckled hoarsely, watching the dog attack the food, then lick the empty metal dish clean. He filled the dog's water dish with fresh cool well water, pouring the clear liquid from a white plastic gallon milk container. "You ate so goddarn fast, Judas, you couldn't have tasted any of it. But you're some good old boy, aren't you." The dog wagged his bushy tail, while licking the sides of his mouth continuously with a curving, pink tongue. Then the retired farmer moved back from the water dish as the dog slurped it dry, getting his muzzle soaking wet, which he licked with his tongue again. "How about if I let you loose, Judas, and we have a look around the place? Just to make sure we don't have an unwanted guest hiding in one of these buildings. Got to

get some peace of mind, before I go to bed tonight. Can't stay up all night worrying myself silly."

Morley Rockland knelt and unsnapped the chain from the big dog's collar. Smiling with satisfaction, he watched the animal take off with long-legged strides in a frenzy of speed at being free of the chain, running first one way and then the other. Tail wagging like a speeded-up metronome, nose skimming the grass like a vacuum sweeper on a rug, Judas barked his excitement in loud, deep-throated, continuous bursts.

"Come on back here, Judas, boy. You're supposed to follow me. We're going to do some looking around," Morley Rockland shouted hoarsely, but with a satisfied smirk slanting his wide-lipped mouth. He shuffled over bare ground to the packing shed and opened the wooden door, its hinges squeaking loudly, to let Judas inside. The dog circled the empty benches and sniffed the plank floor, finally prancing out at his master's command.

Judas barked and whined and wagged his two-foot-long tail continuously as he approached the tractor shed, then slipped in between the two sagging doors. And once inside the dark shed, he moved swiftly over the earthen floor and around the sagging roof beams of the once functional building, empty now, the tractors having been sold off five years back.

The active big dog sniffed out the chicken coop, his back rubbing against the elevated chicken wire, then the empty silo that didn't have a crowned top on it anymore, and the one-car garage that contained a rusting Chevy relic, its tires flat, engine dead. Judas circled the car and sniffed the tires, lifting a hind leg and urinating on each one, before coming back out into the warm daylight.

They inspected the cow barn last, its stalls empty, with decaying straw and hay and animal manure still on the dirt floor. The barn's musty-smelling air was

cool. Rays of yellow light streaked in through cracks in the vertical side boards. Chirping barn swallows flew back and forth between the rafters, indifferent to the intrusion below.

"Nobody around this old barn, Judas. Come on, let's go on back to your doghouse. You had your fun and exercise. And your dinner. I still got to get mine. Not that I need it. Don't do much work to speak of anymore, do I?" Grunting, Morley Rockland stroked the wiry fur on the dog's rump.

At the doghouse, he hooked Judas to his clanking chain, patted him on his furry head, then stood up and admonished the dog, "Now you better keep an eye on things, you hear, Judas, boy? And you better keep those sharp, pointed ears cocked. Don't want to be surprised by that young weirdo. Got to be ready for him when he shows his nigger face around here. I got a surprise planned for him, if he thinks he's going to barbecue us. I'll put the fear of God in his crazy brains first, after we catch him. Then we call the police. Right, Judas?"

The big animal barked and whined and jumped and tugged with all his strength to get free of the taut chain.

The tired farmer grunted his satisfaction and approval at the excited state of the watchdog, then turned away abruptly, shuffling back toward the farmhouse across the rear yard area that was now more weeds and bare earth than grass.

Exhausted from the hiking and the peach tree climbing back at the orchard, Little Oscar had dragged himself along until he made it to the same place off Creek Road that he and his mother had arrived at during the previous December Friday, when first approaching his grandparents' farm. The same two top wooden rails were missing from the split-rail fencing, and were still on the ground nearby, as before when his mother

had pointed them out to him that fateful day over six months ago. But he was glad to see them now. He was back—at last. And he could see the aging, dull red farm outbuildings up ahead some thousand feet or more away, with the upper portion of the gray farmhouse and its colorless cedar shake roof visible above the lower-level farm improvements. It wasn't a pretty sight, but it was surely a welcome one.

Since it was still daylight, with the sun an orange-colored basketball draped precariously on the western horizon, sending angled horizontal rays of sunlight across the rolling, green countryside, Little Oscar decided to stop and rest there by the fence and study the farm until dusk, before approaching the outbuildings to set up camp in one of them for the night.

He was on his third peach when he heard a dog's loud barking. It was sharp and strong and came from near the buildings behind the farmhouse. The barking changed from continuous to intermittent, then stopped altogether. And when silence fell over the place again, it spread across the field before him as if it were an invisible blanket of air. But in a short while, to announce the coming of nightfall, field and tree insects took up the banner of noise and began an incessant chorus of chirping and buzzing, with the crickets the easiest to recognize. He watched an early evening bat flutter and dart across the field after unseen flying insects.

It was then that Little Oscar decided he'd better locate the dog first, before bedding down anywhere closer, to insure his not being detected by the animal in the morning. He had work to do the next day and evening. After that, he didn't care if the dog knew he was on the farm.

He donned the backpack, which was half full of peaches, then scooped up his bedding and headed up the sloping field of ankle-high weeds and rye grass,

fighting the slight tug of gravity. A mild evening breeze caressed his face and arms. He didn't stop until he had made it to the tractor shed. Then after peeping around it, and seeing nothing indicating a dog living nearby, he ambled over to the barn, but saw nothing of a dog inside or outside it, either. He reconnoitered the chicken coop, the garage and the silo, but found nothing of a dog in residence. He stopped behind the packing shed and rested a moment. The dog had to be somewhere between the outbuildings and the farmhouse. He decided not to circle around to the front of the shed, instead to climb up on the roof to see if he could spot the dog from up there. If he couldn't locate the dog anywhere outside, it was probably being kept in the farmhouse shed. But he still had to plan around the animal either way.

The packing shed roof sloped toward the rear and was low enough for Little Oscar to toss his gear onto, before using the rear windowsill as a climbing ledge, and inching himself over the edge. Then he crawled slowly and as quietly as possible over the gritty asphalt shingles up to the front of the roof, lay flat on his stomach and peered over the edge at the yard below him.

The dog's head was resting on its front paws, while the animal lay half out of its doghouse a short distance from the front of the packing shed. It was unaware of any intruder.

Little Oscar was relieved to see that the ferocious-looking beast was attached to the wooden doghouse by a heavy chain. But he decided that he would still have to be extra quiet, cautious and careful with a dog on the premises. And it would be too chancy if he slept on the ground or in one of the buildings. He might oversleep. If his grandfather got up early to let the dog loose in the morning, he just might get caught. So Little Oscar decided to stay right there on the roof. The weather was mild with no sign of rain. He'd be more relaxed up

there anyway, and wouldn't have to worry about the big dog.

He backed up and located himself in the middle of the slanted flat roof, out of sight distance from the ground and at an angle that he couldn't be seen from the farmhouse. Then he set up his bedroll for sleeping, and slid quietly inside it, with his backpack nearby. Once settled, he lay still and stared upward at the twinkling stars and the bright three-quarter moon that bathed everything below in its wash of light, creating eerie contrasts of form and shadow across the farm.

Little Oscar studied the starry scene above him for uncounted minutes, hands clasped under his head, elbows fanned outward. "It's gonna be tomorrow night, Mom. Just like I promised you." His voice was barely a whisper. "Didn't come this far to fail." After a silent interlude, he added, "I love you, Mom," and didn't bother to wipe away the twin tears, each one trickling slowly down the opposite temple.

Morley Rockland, who was still dressed in his denim overalls, backed awkwardly out of the bedroom closet carrying a shiny black shotgun in his thickly veined hands. He sat on his side of the bed next to his wife, who was reading from the Bible, dressed in a summer-weight nightgown. The second-floor bedroom was still harboring the day's heat. The screened windows let in more insect noise than cooling breezes past the spread curtains.

Sarah Rockland glanced over at her husband and whined, "Dad, you're not going to keep that thing out, are you? Just because that man said the boy had threatened to come up here and kill us?" She pushed her sliding bifocals back up to the bridge of her long nose, then brushed a wisp of lank white hair away from her face.

"I have to, Sarah. After I clean and load it, I'll put it down in the shed during the day, then bring it back up

here and keep it in the closet at night. You won't have to look at it."

"Good, I'm glad."

"Got to be ready to scare the shit out of that little squirt, when he shows his nigger face around here. I'll hold him prisoner, while you call the police. We'll get rid of that pest once and for all, after they put the black bastard in jail, with the rest of the hoodlums."

"It's a crying shame we have to worry about such a thing. Our Debbyanne's dead, and now we got her son making trouble for us. Imagine threatening to kill us like that, and bragging about it to that other boy. Don't we deserve a little peace and quiet in our old age? There just don't seem to be any in this wicked world for Bible-reading Christians like us anymore."

"Sure we deserve some peace and quiet. And I aim to get us some with Big Betsy here." Morley Rockland patted the hard, ungiving metal barrel of the twelve gauge shotgun in his lap. "Killed many a rabbit and deer with this hunk of iron. And a mess of groundhogs, too." The old farmer laughed and coughed roughly, then took out his bandana handkerchief and spit a copious glob of phlegm into it.

His wife frowned and turned away. "Just keep that dangerous thing out of my sight. And be careful. You're liable to blow your foot off with it. Can't stand to look at it. Scares the dickens out of me."

"I know that, Sarah. I'll hide Big Betsy under some old clothes on a shelf in the shed. You won't see it. But I want it handy up here at night in the closet. Just don't go poking around in there and you won't touch it, or see it."

"I asked the Lord what we did wrong, getting all this trouble heaped down upon us in our old age. Like sinners and nonbelievers." Sarah Rockland let the Bible flop down flat into her lap. She leaned back deeper into the pillows supporting her shoulders and

head against the bed's pine headboard. "Debbyanne gave us all that trouble growing up. Then ran away and got herself in a family way by a black boy, yet. And then actually coming back here and having that mixed baby down on the greasy tractor shed dirt floor like a common she-goat. Why us—I asked the Lord. And we still can't show our faces to decent folks."

"We didn't do nothing wrong, Sarah. So don't go blaming yourself about past family history. And we can too show our faces to anybody we damn well please. We can sit in church with the best of them."

"Still it hurts. What Debbyanne did to us. And now her boy wanting to kill us."

"You just keep on reading your Bible, Sarah. And let me take care of the young menace. We're holding two aces up our sleeves. Mean and nasty Judas outside, and Big Betsy here inside. That dog can hear a mouse come onto this property. He'll bark like hell at the first step that boy makes on our ground."

"I sure hope you're right, Dad. I've been a nervous wreck ever since that social worker brought the bad news."

"You just calm down, Sarah. You got Judas with his sharp ears, and me with this hunk of iron. We won't let any harm come to you. That nigger crud isn't going to barbecue us like a couple of hot dogs. He's got another think coming, if he tries to pull that off. We're going to stop him right in his tracks. You'll see."

"You better, if we want to go on living."

Morley Rockland tapped the double-barreled shotgun again and nodded his head in silent agreement.

Sarah Rockland took off her rimless bifocals and laid them on the night table next to the bed. Then she rubbed the bridge of her angled nose. "When you're finished fooling with that thing, put out the light on your side. I'm tired, I need to get my beauty rest." She

snapped off the lamp on the night table and laid the Bible next to its ceramic base. "Good night, Dad."

"Good night, Sarah. And don't you worry about nothing."

"How can I help not worrying?"

"I know, I know, Sarah, just try."

And when his wife didn't reply, Morley Rockland turned his attention to the weapon in his lap. He swabbed the bores of both barrels with a piece of oily cloth, pushing it through with a narrow metal rod. When finished, he loaded two shotgun shells into the rear of the barrels, then closed them into the stock and clicked on the safety. "Now I'm ready for our grandson," he mumbled, walking toward the closet.

"Thank the Lord," his wife said, turning onto her side.

Morley Rockland didn't reply, just laughed hoarsely.

Chapter 5

Little Oscar blinked himself awake, stretching his arms out stiffly, then straightening his legs inside the cocoonlike sleeping bag. But he quickly remembered where he was and placed a palm over his spreading mouth, stifling a yawn. It was already warm on the roof, with the sun's rays heating his head. His matted, ruglike hair felt hot to touch. He couldn't remember the last time he had combed or washed it. Then he knuckled the sleep out of his eyes, fingering the crusty residue out of the corners. Finally he lay still and collected his thoughts, reviewing his plans for the daylight hours and for later that night. There would be no more delays now. This was going to be it. He giggled quietly to himself, again using a palm to cover his mouth.

When he heard the rear shed door to the farmhouse open, followed by a slow shuffling of footsteps in his direction, Little Oscar stiffened, placing his arms at his sides, looking like a prone statue. He listened for clues, and instantly recognized his grandfather's familiar

hoarse voice, which sounded extra harsh in the morning's quiet air, when the old farmer called out the watchdog's name. Judas jumped and paced and tugged noisily at the chain. Little Oscar imagined the entire greeting scene below him from the sounds he heard.

"Hey there, Judas, boy, how are you this fine summer morning?"

The watchdog whined and barked its recognition of its master.

"How about we take a good look around again today? Just to make sure nobody's on the place who shouldn't be. And you can sniff everything three times to your heart's content."

Little Oscar sucked in his lower lip, his eyelids narrowed. His grandfather sure talked nicer to a stupid dog than he did to his mother and him last December.

The door hinges to the shed squeaked below him, followed by the dog's paw patter on the wooden floor inside. But he was secure on the slanted roof above, safely out of the range of the dog's sensitive nose and ears; and of his grandfather's watchful eyes as long as he remained still and flat on his back, and the old man didn't go walking behind the shed to inspect its roof from that lower angle. All he had to do was wait out the morning inspection, then get down on the ground and begin his preliminary work for the night's torching. He'd planned it for so long that he got a sudden thrill just thinking about how close he was to seeing it come true. And he could only hope his mother was as excited about it as he was, being up in heaven and looking down on him there on the packing shed roof.

When Morley Rockland returned to the farmhouse, he opened the shotgun and extracted the two exposed buckshot shells, dropping them into his right overalls pocket. Then he covered the heavy weapon with ragged, soiled towels on a wooden shelf next to the house shed's

outside door, before shuffling into the kitchen. His first sniff told him his wife was frying eggs and bacon and the perked coffee was ready for drinking. It didn't matter, summer or winter, he had to have his coffee in the morning. He dropped heavily into his favorite kitchen chair, the one with the back spoke missing, which was located next to the side window. From there he could observe some of the outbuildings and Judas, who was sitting up on his haunches in front of his doghouse, alert and ready for action. It made him feel better about their situation. He had an ally, Judas, the meanest son-of-a-bitch he'd ever seen.

"No sign of the little nigger squirt yet, Sarah. Checked every damn building out there with Judas. That dog sniffed so much, must've worn out his nose. But we didn't find a thing, as usual. Maybe that kid is nowhere near us? Just maybe he got himself lost? And maybe we don't have to worry so much now—not for a while yet, anyway. But if he does show up, Judas'll hear him and start barking like hell. You can bet your life on that."

"You know that dog better'n I do, Dad. But I still think we should watch out for him," Sarah Rockland replied, plopping two sizzling fried eggs onto the chipped ceramic plate in front of her husband. Then she dropped three slices of partially burnt crisp bacon alongside the eggs. "Can't be too careful, when it comes to a kid who ain't exactly right in the head, wanting to burn up his grandparents."

"All right, Sarah, I'll take another look around later on today, after I feed Judas. It'll give his nose some more exercise."

"You had the shotgun with you?"

"Just brought it along to scare the shit out of the pain-in-the-neck, if I caught him. You know, Sarah, get him to stare down both barrels and give him a good look at death."

"Hope you put it away."

"It's in the shed for now."

"Not loaded, I hope."

"Nope, got the shells in my pocket."

"I won't relax till you put it back in the bedroom closet—unloaded—for good."

"Maybe we can do that sooner than we think, Sarah. Straite got us all worried yesterday for nothing. That kid can't be close. Remember, his mother only brought him up this way once, back in last December. So tell me he still remembers how to get up here." Morley Rockland finished the last of his eggs, wiping the yellow yolk off the plate with a hunk of his toasted rye bread, then drank the last of his coffee, before his wife had a chance to sit and eat her breakfast.

"Good God, you finished already? No wonder you always have indigestion."

"Eating's the only thing I enjoy doing these days."

"It's showing. You're getting a potbelly. Pretty soon I'll have to let out your overalls."

Morley Rockland grunted and shrugged his bare shoulders under the denim straps, then got up and poured himself another cup of coffee from the electric pot on the kitchen counter. When he returned to the table, he sipped the hot brew in silence, watching the outbuildings and Judas. He was pleased to see that the dog was still up on his haunches, ears pointing alertly upward, looking mean and hostile like a good watchdog should.

Little Oscar remained on the roof of the packing shed and ate three peaches from his stock of six. Then leaving his gear on his roof headquarters, he climbed down as quietly as possible from the lower rear end. With Judas stationed in front of the packing shed, he decided to look elsewhere for burning materials, always

keeping the other outbuildings between him and the dog.

He squeezed into the tractor shed from the back end of it, after slowly pulling aside a half-rotted siding board. Once inside the building's semidarkness, he had to use his flashlight to see under the dangerously sagging roof. Sticky cobwebs clung to his head and face. Tiny gnats tried to crawl up his nostrils. He watched a brown field mouse scurry across his path on the damp earthen floor as he searched in a crouched position. He was delighted when he found piles of old canvas and oily rags, dragging them over to the rotted board entry for easy access to them later that night. The separate canvas sections and numerous rags smelled of mold and greasy oil, but were dry enough for burning, that was all that mattered to him. When he spotted a rusty, two-gallon metal can, he picked it up and shook it. He could hear liquid splashing around inside the container. Its weight indicated the can was at least half full, and he had to use all of his strength to unscrew the rusty cap. A sweetish odor lifted out of the round opening. Gasoline! Now he had something to help him get the fire going fast. The canvas and rags would burn like newspaper, after getting doused with gasoline. He giggled his glee at such an unexpected find, leaving the can next to the piled canvas and rags.

When he left the tractor shed, he replaced the vertical siding board and made it look as if he'd never been inside the roof-sagging building. Then he searched the chicken coop, but to no avail. He entered the roofless silo through a hole near its bottom, but found nothing. And he came up empty in the open-spaced, slatted corn-crib also. He tried the barn last, finally deciding to use the boards that separated the stalls for firewood. They came away easily enough from their posts. He had a large number of the dry, flat, splintery boards piled in the rear of the barn next to a door, spreading them out

on the dirt floor, covering them with the hay and straw available, some of which was dry, some damp and moldy where the leaking roof had dripped water. He wanted to camouflage the boards in case his grandfather came into the barn with the dog.

Satisfied with his handiwork, he left the barn and returned to his roof headquarters over the packing shed and ate his last three peaches.

Lying on top of his sleeping bag, he rested, waiting for his grandfather to come and release the dog, Judas, to check out the buildings again before it got dark, which gave him plenty of time to think about what he was going to do later that night. He relished the exciting anticipation of getting revenge against his grandparents. Come nighttime, he was going to teach them a lesson. They killed his mother, and they were going to pay for that with their own lives.

"I'm ready, Mom," Little Oscar said in a whispery voice, "you're gonna get your wish tonight, just like I promised."

He closed his eyes and saw his mother's pretty face, with her nice, clean-smelling blonde hair hanging down by her clear, soft-skinned cheeks, and her even, white-toothed friendly smile. Not the ugly, sweaty, scrunched up, sunken-cheeked face he wanted to forget, after she got sick and suffered for so long, then died so pitifully quick. Pretty and happy, that's how he wanted to remember her. And he would always love her—always.

Morley Rockland brought out the daily heaping plate of canned dog food and table scraps and the plastic gallon jug of cool well water to refill the water dish for Judas, then waited nearby for the animal to eat all of the food and drink his fill of the fresh water. Afterwards he released the dog from the link chain and together they checked out the buildings. But the one thing different in the routine, the aged farmer let the

dog enter the buildings alone. He didn't step past the open doorways to inspect the interiors himself, depending instead on Judas' sense of smell to detect a human presence in any of the buildings. He just stood with the loaded shotgun pointing at the ground in front of his feet when he peeked into the barn to watch the dog sniff out the stalls in the long, high-ceilinged farm building. But when Judas didn't flush out anything or anyone of significance, disregarding his lengthy sniffing along the earthen floor in the back of the barn as only the smelling of rodent tracks, he returned the dog to his doghouse chain and patted him on the head for doing his usual good job. Then he returned to the farmhouse, put the unloaded shotgun away on the shed shelf and dropped the shells into his pocket again, finally shuffling into the kitchen and stopping next to the table.

"I told you it was just a scare alarm, Sarah. Judas would've found that mental case by now, if he was hiding in one of the sheds, or the barn. That dog sniffs everything three times or more. Sucks up the smells like a vacuum cleaner. Doesn't miss a spot. That runt can't hide anyplace on this farm, without Judas picking up his scent and flushing him out like a covey of quail."

"I'm glad you're so sure, Dad, 'cause I'm not. But sit down and eat, and don't swallow so much air. You'll burp all night," Sarah Rockland said, carrying a full agate pot past her husband and placing it on a low metal stand in the center of the wooden kitchen table.

Morley Rockland shrugged and dished himself out a plateful of the chuck meat and vegetable stew, then buttered a slice of rye bread. "I'll bring the shotgun back upstairs tonight and keep it in the closet," he began, while chewing his first mouthful of food, "I want it to be handy, in case Judas sounds the alarm."

"Just keep it out of my sight."

"Don't worry, Sarah, I will, I will." After another mouthful of food, Morley Rockland added, "I think we can relax tonight, and watch some TV. And get some sleep, later, too. We don't have to worry about that boy coming here, not yet, anyway. And we got mean Judas watching out for us like a sharp-eared cop. I say that kid can't be near here. Probably can't even find the place."

Sarah Rockland frowned behind owlish bifocals and fixed her plate with heaping globs of the brownish-looking vegetable and chuck meat stew, then sat down and began to eat slowly, watching her husband gobble the stew off his plate as if he were rushing to go put out a fire. When was he going to learn to eat slower? When he was six feet under? She shook her head and concentrated on the food before her. Soon, the only sounds in the kitchen were of two elderly people chewing, with their loose false teeth clicking occasionally.

The moon was out again at three-quarter-full and bright, like a phosphorescent tennis ball suspended in the black sky. It spread enough light below on earth that Little Oscar could easily see the buildings around him. He didn't need to use his flashlight outside, only when in the tractor shed, gathering up the canvas and the oily rags and the half-filled gasoline can.

He circled the outbuildings quickly, but stepping silently with his sneakers on the grass and dirt, always keeping out of sight and earshot of the dog, getting to the farmhouse undetected by the guarding animal.

Along the south side of the dwelling, he deposited half of the canvas and the rags, taking the rest to the wooden front porch. Then he returned to the outbuildings, entering the rear door of the barn, where he used his flashlight to help him gather an armful of the stall slats, carrying them back out the rear barn door, cir-

191

cling beyond the sight and hearing of the dog to the south side of the farmhouse again. Once there, he got on his hands and knees and dragged the boards with him under the living room section, which was supported by low stone piers, offering easy access into the crawl space underneath that front portion of the farmhouse. All he had to do was to push in the three-foot-wide wooden lattice ventilation screening with his feet, which, he noted mentally, would make good fire-starting material, once doused with gasoline.

When on the north side of the farmhouse, facing Judas, but still hidden from the watchdog by the concealing section of lattice screening on that side, he carefully and quietly piled the barn slats against the floor joists and the lattice work, dousing all of it generously with gasoline.

After he had the three sides ready for torching, it left just the rear section of the dwelling unprepared. The kitchen and the dining room had a full cellar under them, but the rear shed behind the kitchen didn't. He could get a fire going under the shed, which would spread to the kitchen and take care of that part of the house. He wanted all four sides of the building going up together. It would insure trapping his grandparents inside the burning house and roasting them like sizzling hot dogs on a barbecue grill. He giggled at the mental picture in his head, vividly seeing his fat, white-haired grandparents tied to a grill and tormented by the red-hot coals below them.

He had used up all the gasoline and prepared the rear shed for burning with newspaper and cardboard found in a metal garbage can nearby and some smaller scraps of wood.

Later, after the flames had caught and spread quickly through each pile, Little Oscar kept making the rounds to ensure their continued burning, at least until he was satisfied they were strong enough to burn

on their own without any help from him. And in a short while the flames started to consume the wood on the structure itself, spreading into a full-fledged house fire. Tongues of orange and yellow and red climbed the clapboard walls like dragon fire. He giggled at his success. It was beautiful and deadly. Soon the whole house would be one big bonfire, and his grandparents wouldn't have a chance of escaping. He got a thrill at the thought.

"It's burning, Mom. See—it's burning, just like I promised you it would," Little Oscar said aloud into the building roar of the fire. He stood back from the growing heat, as the unimpeded flames climbed higher and higher up the tinderlike clapboard walls. He wanted to shout his joy at getting all four piles burning at nearly the same time. The front porch was already half consumed, with the fire working into the front wall of the farmhouse. The draft-whipped flames lit up the darkness like a lighted land beacon. His fires were raising havoc on the hated farmhouse, and so quickly. He was amazed at how quickly.

"Burn, burn, burn," Little Oscar said to himself, as the flames reached the second floor, scorching, smoking, then flaming brightly like a Roman candle. He wrung his hands, hurrying the fire along, anticipating the holocaust. For only then would he feel one hundred percent certain that he was going to accomplish his mission, killing his grandparents, as he had told Spider he would just a few weeks ago.

When Sarah Rockland woke up, she sniffed smoke. Each breath she took was followed by a gasping for clean, clear air, then a back-bending raspy coughing and choking. She groped in the dark and snapped on the night table lamp by the bed. She shook her husband, hollering, "Dad, Dad, wake up! The bedroom's full of smoke. The house must be on fire." She sucked

bitter-tasting smoke into her mouth with each word she spoke. Choking again, she coughed out the acrid taste. "Oh, my God! Dad, look, the fire's shooting up past the window," she added, pounding on her husband's back. Then she fell into another coughing and hacking spell, while banging her husband awake with her fists.

"What the hell? Where's all this smoke coming from?" Morley Rockland bellowed hoarsely like an angry bull, and fell into a coughing spasm himself.

"I told you we still weren't safe from that crazy kid," Sarah Rockland said, her voice raising to a banshee wail. "But you said not to worry."

"The little squirt's here? How? . . ."

"Never mind how, Dad. We've got to get out of here." Sarah Rockland struggled off the bed on her side like a two-legged hippopotamus.

Morley Rockland rolled off the bed on his side and landed on all fours. "Goddarn it!" He righted himself and rubbed the burning smoke out of his eyes, which only made the feeling get worse. Then he shuffled around the bed to his wife's side, and together they marched like two drunks, bumping hips, arm-in-arm, toward the bedroom door. But when they opened it, a blast of flames met them headfirst, as if shot out of a flamethrower. The shocking wall of fire drove them back into the bedroom, with arms raised to protect their faces from the searing heat.

"What are we going to do now, Dad? We'll burn to death, if we don't get out of here!" Sarah Rockland's voice rose to an hysterical pitch by the last word.

"Let's try the windows, Sarah. We still got a chance. Calm yourself."

They coughed more smoke out of their lungs backtracking to the side window, where the flames climbing up the outside wall drove them away from that escape opening. At the front window, over the lower-level front porch, which was completely in flames with the fire eat-

ing a ten-foot-wide path into the front wall, their escape was sealed off from that exit. The intense heat forced them back once more. They retreated to the middle of the bedroom, where Sarah Rockland dropped in a bulky lump to the oval area rug that covered most of the wooden bedroom floor, which was already hot on her legs. She pulled the sheet off the bed and wrapped it around her head, the rest draping downward to the rug underneath her. Morley Rockland remained standing, his hands over his mouth and nose to keep out the smoke when he breathed, which was getting more difficult with each passing second. His eyes watered from the burning sensation. He watched the curtains catch fire and flash into yellow-orange flame and disintegrate in seconds. He winced and blinked rapidly to rid his eyes of smoke, but it only added to the irritation. His vision was blurred. He squinted to see. His chest hurt to breathe. And his wife's hopeless figure before him on the floor looked ghostly, surrounded by the thickening gray smoke.

"Dad, do something!" Sarah Rockland shouted above the roar of the fire. "Oh, dear God, I can't breathe anymore. We're going to be burned to death." Her sobs shook her broad back. Her head was bent forward, as if in prayer, the sheet still covering her completely. "Oh, dear God, somebody save us!" she screamed. A moment later, she added, "Dad, do something!"

Morley Rockland didn't reply. He just stood there, with the heat searing his skin till he could hardly keep from screaming himself. He felt like a roasting pig on a spit over a fire. He knew he wouldn't be able to stand it much longer. And when the night table lamp went out, he knew the power line to the house must've melted in the fire. Now the only light in the bedroom came from the blazing inferno that surrounded them, flashing its deadly brightness ironically through the two windows

and the hallway. When the rug they stood on started to smolder, feeling the heat penetrate his bare soles, he knew it would be only minutes before the entire room would be a furnace. Staying alive now meant only more suffering to endure, until consumed entirely by the flames. It was senseless to keep on suffering. There wasn't any hope. Absolutely none.

"I depended on that goddarn animal. Didn't bark once all night." Morley Rockland coughed and spit out the smoky-tasting phlegm on the rug.

"I can't stand the heat anymore. Oh, dear God, my legs are burning up. Do something, Dad, quick!" Sarah Rockland screamed.

"I will, I will," Morley Rockland murmured, shuffling to the bedroom closet where he reached in, then backed out holding the shotgun. After fumbling through the pockets of his overalls left on the chair beside the wall and not far from the bed, he extracted the two shells and loaded the shotgun with them. Then he approached his slumped wife huddled under the white sheet on the smoldering rug, who was now sobbing and screaming like a crazy woman.

Hesitating, feeling the shotgun grow heavier and warmer in his hands, until he couldn't stand her screaming any longer, Morley Rockland raised the weapon to his wife's head and mumbled, "Goodbye, Sarah." Tears flowed freely down his heated face as he squeezed the trigger to the right barrel.

Little Oscar ran around the farmhouse looking like a circus clown being chased by a lion, wide-eyed as a monkey, while sweating profusely in the fire-heated night air. And he no longer cared if the dog saw him. Its barking was drowned out by the fire's roar. He circled the house with impunity, and he didn't care if his grandparents heard the dog barking or saw him from

their bedroom window. It was too late. They couldn't escape now. He couldn't restrain the joy he felt, jumping up and down and clapping his hands as if applauding a stage performance.

"I got 'em now, Mom. They're cooking like a couple of hot dogs. Gonna burn up the rest of the place for you, too."

Little Oscar stood still a moment, giggling and listening to the screaming he heard coming from the second floor. After a loud noise like a truck backfire, the screaming suddenly stopped. A second loud blasting sound followed soon after the first. Then all was silence again up there on the second floor, except for the continuous roar of the flames.

When the rear shed fell in and the kitchen roof followed, along with the fiery collapse of the front porch, and knowing the rest of the house was doomed also, with no chance for escape by his hated grandparents, Little Oscar turned his attention to the outbuildings. He used pieces of burning wood from the shed to ignite fires in all of the other buildings, saving the packing shed nearest the doghouse for last, carefully approaching the panicked dog. He stood just far enough away. The animal strained the metal chain to its limit, trying to get at Little Oscar, who laughed and giggled with glee. And when he threw pieces of burning wood at the packing shed and at the dog, some landed inside the doghouse. Snarling and growling, the frightened animal dodged the erratically tossed missiles. Little Oscar giggled at the dog barking and snapping at the air with its big teeth. When the packing shed roof caved in and part of the wall debris fell against the doghouse, Little Oscar laughed and jumped up and down and clapped his hands in appreciation. He wanted the doghouse and the dog to be burned up along with the rest of the farm and his grandparents. Nothing was to be left. Just him.

He would never forget the blazing scene all around him, burning a picture into his brain, a living negative. Yes—he would never forget it.

"It's all over for them, Mom," Little Oscar said with a wet-lipped giggle. "Got the whole place going up now, just like I promised you."

When Little Oscar heard a distant fire truck siren, he reasoned quickly that some nearby farm neighbor must've spotted the fire and called the rural fire-fighting volunteers. Its siren blare got closer with each passing second. Little Oscar decided to leave. His work was finished. He didn't have to stay to the end.

He returned to where he had his bedroll and back-pack hidden behind the burning outbuildings in the field far enough away to be safe. And after donning the backpack, and holding the sleeping bag and mat roll under his arm, he ran down the inclined field toward the fence opening approach near Creek Road. Once there, he fell to the ground exhausted from his fire-setting efforts and the running. He used the bedroll for a pillow while prostrate on the grass, still listening to the fire truck siren, breathing heavily and feeling a pain in his chest. But he was content now, having accomplished his mother's dream for her, destroying the lousy farm and her unloving parents. He hoped she was as happy about it up in heaven as he was down on earth, watching the fires consume the far-off farm buildings and brightening up the dark sky.

Little Oscar remained a moment longer on the ground. And when he regained his breath, he enjoyed the lull in activity, for he knew he would have to hurry soon and get off the farm property before the fire truck finally got there. But when he heard a metallic rattling accompanied by a thudding, bumping sound, sensing something was being dragged along the ground, getting

closer and louder by the second, he stood up to see just what was causing the strange noises.

"It's Judas," Little Oscar said aloud.

The large beast of a dog was coming toward him at a full gallop, bounding in the open moonlit brightness that flooded the field with its eerie wash of gray-white light, while getting additional light from the fire. The chain, still attached to a piece of board, bounced crazily alongside the animal's flank. When Judas got close enough, Little Oscar could see his fearful flashing teeth, and the gleaming wet tongue dangling between those huge lower fangs.

He threw the bedroll at the animal, but missed short. The dog leaped over it with ease. Little Oscar ran to get the nearest fence railing lying on the ground about ten feet from him. But Judas got to him in one flying leap, landing against his back. Little Oscar ended up face down with grass and dirt smearing his nose. He flipped over in time to grasp the dog's neck and keep its lunging mouth and snapping teeth away, gripping the dog's fur with all his strength. Judas twisted to get free, biting at Little Oscar's arms. The dog's hot, foul breath poured onto his face. The gnashing teeth ripped his arms to shreds. The pain was instant and sharp. His own blood dripped into his mouth, wet, warm and saline. When his arm strength weakened, then gave way completely, the dog's fangs closed quickly on Little Oscar's neck like a vice clamping shut, with those big, knife-sharp teeth sinking easily into his soft flesh, penetrating deep into his throat as if they were long spikes. The pain was mercifully brief.

Little Oscar's arms fell to his sides. He tried to breathe, but couldn't, with Judas' hold on his neck.

He couldn't scream, nor could he move. The darkness around him gradually became total, despite his eyes being open, while the snarling dog shook him by the neck as if he were a limp rag. He couldn't feel the

pain anymore. But his brain remained momentarily active. He saw his mother, young and blonde and pretty. She was smiling at him. He wanted to tell her, "Mom, I still love you," seeing the words flash across the mental screen in his head, just before the lights went out. The last sense to leave him was his hearing, with Judas' snarling loud in his ears, until that too dimmed to a faint echo, then total silence.

EPILOGUE

The police had to shoot Judas to get at Little Oscar's mutilated body. They buried the dead dog in the field behind the destroyed farm buildings. After the firemen had recovered the Rocklands' charred remains, they were subsequently buried in their family plot in a church cemetery on the Pleasanton-Mt. Lebanon Road some three miles from the burnt-out farm. Not all of their far-flung, grown children attended the services the following week. As for Little Oscar, the same mortician who officiated at his mother's funeral, handled his. And through the cosmetic miracles of mortuary science, Little Oscar's fang-ripped body was restored to a presentable condition, then buried next to his mother in the public cemetery outside Capital City, with Carl Straite and Mrs. Harris attending his burial. The Wednesday morning when he was buried turned out mild and sunny with a soft, hair-mussing breeze, an unusually dry, pleasant July day for the humid eastern seaboard. Just the opposite from that cold raw day

when they buried his mother. Only this time, Mrs. Harris left the cemetery alone in the county car, preoccupied with thoughts of either having a backyard picnic, and inviting some neighbors over, or driving to the shore. Her children loved the boardwalk and the amusement pier rides. Carl Straite left the cemetery equally indecisive about after-work plans, whether to play tennis or to go golfing to take advantage of such beautiful weather. Following the hasty departures, the grounds keepers dispatched Little Oscar into his grave and the waiting backhoe quickly filled it with dirt, all within less than a half hour. Once again in his short life it was total darkness for Little Oscar. But at least now he was resting in peace next to his mother. The only adult he ever truly loved and trusted completely—without reservation—and with his life.

ABOUT THE AUTHOR

In order to write the novel, **LITTLE OSCAR**, Carmen Anthony Fiore had to return emotionally to his social worker life on the streets and in the various homes located in the ghettos of New Jersey where he tried to alleviate crisis after crisis for his client mothers and their fatherless children; and to his constant dismay, he was not always successful. Later, as a sixth grade teacher in a ghetto school in Trenton, New Jersey, he was half social worker and half school teacher and often full-time disciplinarian while trying to teach the basics of education to his unruly students. His urban background and experiences could not be denied nor ignored and out of them came the characters who live and die in **LITTLE OSCAR**.

After a 13-year sojourn in the rolling farmland and wooded countryside of Hunterdon County, New Jersey where he helped raise two children into adulthood while pursuing his writing career, Carmen Anthony Fiore now lives with his wife, who is a landscape and floral artist, in suburban Mercer County, New Jersey.

His other published works include the critically acclaimed, prize-winning novel, **THE BARRIER**, plus a novel of suspense set in the exotic south of Italy, **VENDETTA MOUNTAIN**, and a number of short stories. He is presently co-authoring a work of nonfiction about Italian-American women and their twentieth century experiences as daughters of the immigrants.

Another good read from **TOWNHOUSE PUBLISHING.**

THE BARRIER

by

Carmen Anthony Fiore

THE BARRIER is a strong-tasting antidote for reader complacency and hazy eyestrain from reading too much predictable formula fiction. As social commentary, the novel took a hard look at America's national welfare system and found it wanting when first published in a hardcover edition to critical acclaim in 1964.

And it is obvious to those who are aware of what is going on in America that nothing has really changed in our decaying older cities.

THE BARRIER'S staying power likens it to a literary time capsule that refuses to be dated. It accurately predicted a bloated welfare bureaucracy that would become destructive to blacks and whites, rampant crime in our urban streets, welfare fraud, unwed mothers breeding more unwed mothers (and numerous sons) by invisible fathers, and schools that would remain ineffective. The current flood of daily newspaper articles and weekly magazine reports attest to America's growing failure to control crime against its people and property and to stop drug trafficking, while our city schools graduate functional illiterates by the thousands every June.

Sensing a need to keep this important book before the concerned reading public, Townhouse Publishing has reprinted **THE BARRIER** in a quality paperback format on acid-free paper priced at only $4.95 per copy.

The author witnessed the urban turmoil of the fifties and sixties firsthand in New Jersey's depressed neighborhoods as a social worker and later as an elementary school teacher. And out of these jarring experiences was born the character Bobbie Lee, the youthful antihero of **THE BARRIER** who typifies the black youth in trouble with a dominant adult white society. There was no place for Bobbie Lee then, and the change has been negligible for the present-day Bobbie Lees who won't go away, staying to haunt us until there is *real* progress.

THE BARRIER is your unique vehicle into a different and interesting world where you will gain new insights about *them* and yourself. Take the trip. You will like yourself better for having done so.

---

185 pages   ISBN 0-939219-01-8 $4.95 per copy

Order from: **TOWNHOUSE PUBLISHING,**
    301 N. Harrison Street
    Bldg.-B, Suite 115, Princeton, NJ 08540

Please send _____ copy(s) of **THE BARRIER** to:

Name _____

Address _____ City _____ State _____ Zip _____

Check or money order only. Do not send cash through the mails.

All books shipped postpaid.